The Dante Inferno:

Forever Dante: Lucia

*The Dante Dynasty Series:
Book #11*

by

Day Leclaire

USA Today Bestselling Author

Please Note

This is a work of fiction. Names, characters, places, and incidents either are the product of the author's imagination or are used fictitiously, and any resemblance to actual persons, living or dead, business establishments, events or locales is entirely coincidental.

Cover Design by Melyssa Naujoks January 2020

ISBN-13: 978-1-939925-42-8

For more information, please visit my website: http://www.DayLeclaire.com

Thank You.

Book Description

*Some blazes, once ignited, can't be
extinguished.
Just one burning touch connects a Dante
with his soul mate.
The Inferno ... curse or blessing?*

One scorching touch connects love child Lucia
Moretti with protective bodyguard, Ty
Masterson. One passionate night together
changes their lives forever. One painful secret
will tear them apart and threaten to destroy
both their lives.

All love child Lucia Moretti has ever wanted is
to share her father's name. To be a Dante, like
her dad. To belong. To feel the burn of The
Inferno when she first joins hands with her
soul mate. Unfortunately, she no longer
believes in fairy tales. Or so she thinks until a
protective stranger touches her and The
Inferno blazes through her. Too bad he
doesn't feel it, too.

Ty Masterson is hired to protect Lucia when
the Dantes are attacked at their spectacular
gala. Then tragedy strikes and he must protect

Lucia with his life, all the while fighting the passion that explodes between them.

But who is Ty, really? And why does a strange mark appear on his hand . . . and an identical one on Lucia's? When dire circumstances force them to marry, they face a choice. To honor their marriage vows and accept the blessing of The Inferno . . . or part ways forever and risk its curse.

Dedication

To my readers with my sincere apology for the interminable delay getting this book to you. Thank you so much for your unending support of The Dante Dynasty. Your patience, encouragement, and enthusiasm have meant the world to me!

All my love and gratitude to Adrienne Glendening Smith for being my eyes and brain during the editing process. You are the heart of our family!

Table of Contents

.

Other Titles by Day Leclaire

The Dante Inferno:
The Dante Dynasty Series

Some blazes, once ignited, can't be extinguished. Just one burning touch connects a Dante with his soul mate. The Inferno ... curse or blessing?

Sev's Blackmailed Bride, Book #1

Marco's Stolen Wife, Book #2

Nicolò's Wedding Deception, Book #3

Lazz's Contract Marriage, Book #4

Luc's Unwilling Wife, Book #5

Rafe's Temporary Fiancée, Book #6

Draco's Marriage Pact, Book #7

Gianna's Honor-Bound Husband, Book #8

Becoming Dante: Gabe, Book #9

Dante's Dilemma: Romero, Book #10

Forever Dante: Lucia, Book #11

Chapter One

"*Face it, Gabe.* The Inferno doesn't work. Not for me. My palm is broken or something." Lucia shook her hand as though she actually hoped it would magically flare to life. Not that it did. Far from it. She laughed, praying her twin brother didn't detect the heartbreak beneath the sound. "Or maybe I'm the one who's broken."

Now that was closer to the truth.

Her brother frowned. "You're not broken and neither is The Inferno. You just haven't met the right person, yet."

"That's easy for you to say. You did meet the right person."

Lucia glanced over her shoulder in the direction of her sister-in-law, Kat, who cradled their eight-week-old son, Matteo, in her arms. The two stood at the far end of the hallway on the executive level of Dantes, surrounded by Dante men. Everyone had gathered for a meeting to discuss security for the upcoming gala, including her boss, Primo, the family patriarch. But children and family always came first with them, so Matteo took precedence over the meeting.

Of course, her brother Gabe, along with Kat and Matteo, were all Dantes now, adopted by the family who'd taken them into their hearts once they'd discovered the family black sheep, Dominic, had fathered a son out of wedlock. Gabe had even legally changed his last name to Dante at the request of Dominic's father, Primo.

He now had both a grandmother and grandfather, four half-brothers, and another four cousins. What none of the Dantes knew was that Gabe had a twin sister, a secret Lucia insisted he keep until she chose whether or not to reveal the truth.

"You can tell them, you know," he said in an undertone. "They'll accept you the same way they accepted me."

She shook her head before he'd even finished speaking. "I'm not ready. I may never be ready."

"Lucia, how can you not be ready? You've wanted to be a Dante your entire life."

"No," she whispered, fighting to keep all emotion from her voice.

Something tickled her nerves just then, like a feather-light touch stroking the length of her spine. It distracted her, had her looking around, attempting to locate the source of the disturbance. With a shrug, she returned her attention to her brother.

"Once upon a time I wanted to be a Dante," she conceded. "That dream died long ago. Fairy tales don't exist. And only a very few lucky people experience lives that end happily ever after. I'm not one of them. I never have been. To be perfectly honest, I have no interest in ever falling in love again, let alone marrying."

"I felt the same way," Gabe retorted, the words filled with a harsh intensity. "Hell, I never bought into all that fairy tale shit our father tried to sell us. Not ever. Not until—"

His gaze shifted toward his wife and everything about him softened. Strengthened. A bright light seared his odd, golden Dante eyes and he dug his thumb into the center of his palm, rubbing at the itch that resulted from The Inferno.

She doubted he even realized it. The itch was part of the Dante myth and mystique, one she'd spent a lifetime wishing she could experience. They called it The Inferno, the intense burning connection a Dante shared with his or her soul mate when they first joined hands.

The burning itch never truly subsided, but lingered from that day onward as a perpetual reminder of their love. It marked them, branded them—not visibly, but on some spiritual level, filling them with a bone-deep *knowing,* the awareness that this person was the one. Their mate. A love that would last forever and a day. Lucia had spent her entire life longing for The Inferno to strike, until finally, she'd given up hope of it ever happening.

Before Gabe could offer any further argument, a strange awareness teased her senses again, more intensely this time and she fought to stand perfectly still instead of spinning around in a circle and searching for the cause.

She forced herself to focus on her brother and their conversation. They didn't have much time. Sharing a few private moments with her twin, one that wouldn't give her away to the Dantes, were few and far between.

"I'm happy for you, Gabe," she insisted. "I really am. But your fairy tale ending isn't mine."

"I was wrong about the Dantes. Wrong about The Inferno."

She smiled, attempting to inject a hint of lightness into the intensity of the moment. "Did you just say you were wrong? Good Lord.

It's only taken you thirty years to use the "w" word, but I've finally lived long enough to hear you admit what I've know from the moment we were born." She waited until he returned her smile before adding, "Face facts, Gabe. What's right for you isn't right for me. I'm not a real Dante, and I never will be."

He challenged her with a single look. "Then why did you go to work for Primo? Why apply for a job with our grandfather if you didn't still long to be part of the Dante world?"

Her gaze slid away and she toyed with the teardrop necklace Primo had given her as a combination Christmas gift and bonus. The fire diamond flashed with a smoldering brilliance, a painful echo of The Inferno. Leave it to the Dantes to own the only mines in the world to produce such unique and stunning gemstones, a fitting match for the family blessed—or cursed, depending on who you asked—with The Inferno.

The awareness grew more intense, creating a buzz of excitement. Lucia stiffened, the odd disturbance finally solidifying into a bizarre sort of recognition. She could actually feel his approach. Feel the heated stroke of his gaze on her back, followed by an insistent magnetic tug, one laced with desire.

He's here.

The words echoed in her heart and mind, and took root. She struggled to resist the irresistible, refusing to turn around or look for the source of the attraction. And yet, every nerve in her body demanded she respond. That she acknowledge a dream she'd longed for as a child and rejected as an adult. A dream she'd put aside, like a beloved toy she'd outgrown.

He's here. Take him. Make him yours.

She struggled to pick up the thread of her conversation with Gabe, latching onto it with something akin to desperation. "I told you. When I took the job as Primo's executive assistant, I wanted to get to know our grandfather from a safe distance."

His mouth compressed. "Which is why you used that bastard's name you were married to. You knew Primo would have recognized your maiden name."

"Now neither of us are Morettis." Saying it aloud filled her with a painful sadness. "I'm Lucia Benedict and you're Gabriel Dante."

"I don't know how you can stand to call yourself Benedict."

"Andrew's in the past, Gabe." She didn't dare look at her brother. If she did, she'd lose what little remained of her self-control. "You rescued me from him, and I'll always be grateful."

"I didn't rescue you soon enough." The words escaped, full of pain and regret. "I'm sorry I didn't come for you in time. Before he—"

"He's dead now. He can't hurt me ever again." It amazed her how calmly she could refer to that hideous year, months full of pain and darkness. She shook off the memories. "This isn't the time or place to revisit all of that."

He fought to switch gears, and she smiled sympathetically. Not an easy task. He'd adopted the role of her protector when they were little more than babies. Nothing had changed in all the years since. He glanced toward his wife. Everyone was hugging. Soon they'd head this way, and she needed to put an end to their exchange before anyone thought to question why she and Gabe were indulging in such an intense, private conversation.

She gestured toward the Dantes. "Everyone's planning for a spectacular gala, remember? New Beginnings. You should join your family now. People are going to wonder why you're spending so much time with me."

"First, you are family," he stated in a steely tone. "And second, I'm not going anywhere until you promise you won't give up. Not on The Inferno and not on the Dantes."

Primo glanced their way and she launched into speech. "Fine. I won't give up."

But it was a lie and they both knew it. She *had* given up on The Inferno. It was just a fairy tale. A dream. Wishful thinking, no matter what the Dantes believed. Besides, she wasn't a Dante and never would be. After her father had abandoned them and her subsequent, disastrous marriage, she wanted nothing more to do with love or commitment. Ever.

Apparently, The Inferno felt the same way, giving up on her, just as she'd given up on it.

"That's all I need to hear," Gabe said, apparently deciding to accept her words at face value.

He held out his fist to Lucia, keeping it low and tight against his body so no one would see. He extended his index finger curved to form the shape of a small hook. With a smile, she copied his gesture, linking fingers with him. It was a game the two had played with their mother from the time they were toddlers, their special way to say, "I love you," whenever the other needed strength or support.

"I'm here if you need me," he said, leaning in to give her cheek a quick kiss.

I need you, she almost replied, biting back the words at the last instant. He gave her an odd look, as though catching some part of her aborted comment and she forced a reassuring smile to her lips. "Give Kat my love."

"I will. I guess we'll have to skip our weekly dinner since the gala is tomorrow."

"I'll see you there, instead."

She'd see him, despite not being able to acknowledge their connection. When he'd become a Dante, she'd lost the ability to claim him as her twin. For some reason, that hurt even more than turning her back on love. She could live without a man in her life.

Deep down, she knew she couldn't live without family.

She's here.

The strange words echoed through Ty Masterson, catching him off guard. What the hell? After a momentary hesitation, he followed the group of Dantes down the hallway toward the office of the head honcho.

She's here. Find her.

He froze, not sure what was happening, but automatically scanning the hallway for trouble. Elegance and beauty surrounded him. People went quietly about their business. Nothing sounded off. Nothing felt off.

Okay, it was official. He was losing it.

After a final, cautious check of the area, he followed the group into the sprawling office of their CEO. Dante males filled the room, including the man he assumed was the family patriarch, Primo Dante. And still some part of him remained on alert, sweeping the room for whatever felt so intensely off.

Then he saw her. A gorgeous woman stood outside the circle of males. The instant his gaze settled on her, the words grew louder, more insistent.

She's here. Take her. Make her yours.

She remained off to one side, unnaturally still and contained. It was a façade, he recognized in that instant. A shield of protection. The only question, protection against what?

He ignored the men, even though they were the reason he was attending this meeting, and focused on the woman. She inspired the insidious words pulsating through him, taunting his legendary self-control and threatening to rip it to shreds.

Until this moment, he'd have claimed no woman could ever make him lose control. And yet, one look and she called to him like a siren of old, her seductive song drowning out all thought and reason. He took a single step in her direction, then forced himself to freeze. Forced himself to breathe. Forced himself to examine and evaluate. To depend on logic rather than emotion.

He studied her, attempting to determine on a rational level what made her so irresistible. She was a petite woman, compensating for her lack of inches with sky-high heels. What little there was of her packed a deadly punch. She wore a simple cream, long-sleeved dress that dipped in front just enough to reveal a hint of generous cleavage. The silky material flowed downward, hugging each curve, caressing each dip from generous breasts, to narrow waist, to rounded, womanly hips, before screeching to a halt mid-knee in a ta-dah moment, almost as though to say, "And here are the most spectacular legs you've ever seen."

His gaze shifted upward again, analyzing. It was an occupational hazard that had served him well over the years. Protected him. Allowed him to maintain his loner status and depend only on himself.

She'd contained her hair in a ruthlessly tidy bundle at the nape of her neck. But nothing could control the wayward curls that fought to escape and tumble in a chaotic mass down her back. Nor could the rigid hairstyle conceal the unusual color, a glorious mix of every shade of brown, from bronze to streaks of café au lait, then layers of sable blended with a pale flax that matched her dress. He'd never seen anything like it.

What he could see of her face from across the room suggested true beauty. High, arching cheekbones drew attention to unusual teal colored eyes. One moment he swore they were blue, the next green. A trick of the light, no doubt. Her nose was straight and elegant above a firm chin that hinted at stubbornness. But her mouth gave away her true nature, lush and full and begging to be kissed, even when she attempted to compress it into a severe line.

She chose that moment to turn slightly toward Primo in response to a question. A single teardrop diamond hanging from her neck, exploded in shards of color, echoing the explosion of desire ripping through him.

Take her now!

Ty almost obeyed the unspoken command. Almost charged across the room to sweep her into his arms and carry her off to a private oasis where he'd strip away every bit of artifice, until only the true woman remained. Maybe he would have if Juice hadn't chosen that moment to approach, reminding him of his true purpose.

He'd attended this meeting for business, not to seduce a woman. Time to focus on the job, normally an easy task. Today, not so much.

Juice greeted him with a slap on the back that would have felled a lesser man. "Here he is now," he announced to the room at large, the rumbling bass of his voice overriding all conversation.

In response, one of the Dantes tore himself from the pack and approached. His hitched gait warned of an injury never fully healed. "Luc Dante," he introduced himself, offering his hand. "COO of Dantes Security and Courier Service. I understand from Juice you're the best man to guard our most important assets at the upcoming gala."

Ty acknowledged the compliment with a rare smile, though part of him remained keenly aware of *her*. "The Dante fire diamonds."

Luc lifted an eyebrow. "Actually, I was referring to the women who will be wearing the diamonds."

"Masterson's the most protective man I know," Juice interjected. "He won't let anything happen to his assignment. He'll protect her with his life."

Ty gave it to him straight. "Absolutely. My assignment is my top priority. I don't often assist with this type of work, anymore, but the few jobs I accept, I give my all."

"Not that I've been able to tempt you to accept many. Not now that you're one of the idle rich," Juice ribbed.

Ty shook his head. "I can't take credit for that since it wasn't my doing."

"Other than saving that poor boy from a pair of vicious kidnappers. That was all your doing. And his grandfather was very grateful. Left Ty a tidy inheritance when he passed away a few years ago, including a quasi-mansion in Seacliff." Juice added for Luc's benefit.

Uncomfortable with the direction the conversation had taken, Ty deliberately steered the discussion back to the task at hand. "Anyway, when Juice asked for help . . ." He shrugged. "Let's just say I owe him."

Luc grinned. "You're not the only one. I've lost count of the number of times he's bailed me out of trouble. I'm hoping tomorrow night will be another of those occasions. Thank you for agreeing to help us."

Ty inclined his head. He recognized a former military man when he saw one, and didn't doubt he gave off the same vibe. He'd developed a knack for spotting kindred spirits who'd long ago lost their innocence of the world. Active combat had a way of doing that. The men and women he knew all had a certain attitude. A certain way of regarding the world around them. A certain keenness when it came to the fragility of life and how quickly it can change.

Or end.

"Let me introduce you to everyone, and then we'll make ourselves comfortable in the conference room while we go over logistics." He started at the top. "My grandfather, Primo Dante, the founder of our business."

The older man shot Ty an assessing look from beneath bushy gray brows, his dark eyes alert and discerning, despite his years. Totally disregarding the no smoking regulations, his strong, white teeth clamped around a smoldering cigar. He must have been satisfied with what he saw because he thrust out his hand and gave Ty's a firm shake.

"It is my pleasure to meet you." His voice suited him, rolling out in deep, lyrical waves that contained all the romance and warmth of his Italian homeland. It spoke to Ty on some level he didn't quite understand, weaving a spell around and through him.

"Did you serve with Luc?" Primo asked.

It took a moment for Ty to shake off his response to Primo's voice. What the hell was wrong with him? "No, sir. I brushed up against Juice a time or two, but I didn't have the honor of working with your grandson." He spared Luc a swift glance. "Though, I suspect if we were to compare deployments, we'd discover we've worked in tangent on occasion."

Primo waved his cigar through the air, a fragrant wreath of smoke following in its wake. *"Così è la vita.* Our lives are circles, intersecting and overlapping many other circles, all at God's mysterious direction." Primo's eyes narrowed, sharpened. "You are a man of faith?"

"There are no atheists in foxholes," he quoted. Or possibly misquoted. Not that he'd ever been in an actual foxhole. Foxholes were static combat positions that rarely worked in today's warfare.

Primo snorted and a deep, rolling chuckle erupted from him. It seemed to fill the room with its warmth, intensifying the feeling of coming home. It made no sense at all to Ty. He wasn't even Italian, despite having learned the language during his service.

"Vero," the old man conceded. "But what counts is whether a man remains faithful when he is out of the foxhole and fear is absent."

A man who bore a striking resemblance to Primo interrupted, gently putting an end to the subject. "Sev Dante." He offered his hand, but not his title. Had to be the boss man. "Pleased to have you onboard." He quickly introduced several other Dantes, along with their titles.

That just left the woman. Once again that odd, insistent demand rang through his head, more strident this time. *She's yours. Take her!* Ignoring the voice, his gaze targeted in her direction like a heat-seeking missile. He'd caught her staring. A hint of color touched her cheeks and those stunning teal eyes shifted, clinging to Primo as though he were a safe harbor in stormy seas. Strange.

The old man grinned. "Ah, you have noticed my executive assistant. She is as brilliant as she is beautiful. Allow me to introduce you to Lucia Benedict."

Ty stepped in her direction, an awareness grabbing him in an unbreakable hold. *She's mine!* Capturing her gaze with his, he started to offer his hand, only to be swept away by Juice and Luc.

Juice clapped a huge hand on his shoulder, nearly dislocating it. "Time to get to work, Masterson. You can flirt with the lady another time."

The Inferno didn't work. Lucia stared glumly at her palm. How many times had she told herself that? And yet, here she sat, the fairy tale teasing her. Tempting her. Whispering wicked possibilities in her ear. And all because of Ty Masterson.

Part of her wished she'd had the opportunity to touch him. To see if she felt The Inferno when they shook hands. Another part of her scoffed at the idea. She didn't deserve The Inferno. It had rejected her because she'd rushed into marriage with Andrew Benedict, believing *he* was her Inferno mate, when in fact, nothing could have been further from the truth.

Besides, she didn't want the complications The Inferno would bring. She definitely didn't want a man in her life again. Ever. She'd tried that, and it had been the most painful and terrifying experience of her life.

The door to Primo's private office opened, and he and Nonna entered the reception area where she sat. The pair held hands as they usually did. With unconscious grace, her grandfather lifted his wife's hand to his mouth and planted a lingering kiss in the palm. Unbidden, tears pricked Lucia's eyes at the loving gesture. How she longed to claim them as her own. But she didn't dare. Didn't dare risk losing what little contact she currently enjoyed.

"Lucia, *mio cuore,* I am off to eat lunch with my sweet Nonna," Primo announced.

"I'll see you tomorrow at the gala?"

He heaved a sigh. "Yes. Events have conspired so that we will not meet again until tomorrow night."

Lucia smiled. As much as she'd love to offer a more effusive farewell, she limited herself to saying, "Have a nice time." She stifled a sigh. So banal. So generic, when instead, she longed to leap to her feet and give them both a tight, lingering hug.

Nonna, as she'd insisted she be called, paused by Lucia's desk. "Would you care to join us, Lucia? I would love to get to know you better."

Tempted beyond measure, Lucia hesitated, then reluctantly shook her head. Primo had asked her to fill in for one of the gala's models who'd been forced to cancel at the last minute due to illness. Unable to think of a reasonable excuse, she'd allowed him to pressure her into agreeing.

"I have a final fitting for my gown in forty-five minutes. I want to make sure everything's perfect so your beautiful diamonds are showcased to their best advantage."

"Pfft." Primo swept a hand through the air in clear dismissal. "Everyone will be staring at you, not our fire diamonds. They come a distant second to such a lovely woman."

Nonna laughed. "I would call him a flattering fool, but he is right, my dear. Your beauty quite outshines any gemstone."

Even though she knew they were being ridiculously effusive, she treasured every word her grandparents spoke. Cradled them close. Temptation beckoned, urging her to confess her identity. But she didn't dare. It would change everything and she wasn't quite ready for whatever that change might bring. She'd learned that the hard way. Anticipation never matched reality.

The minute they left, Lucia buried her face in her hands, struggling for control. She couldn't explain her reluctance. Couldn't explain why she hesitated when she'd seen how they'd welcomed Gabe into their fold once they discovered his identity. But she'd trusted once, loved totally and completely, and nearly been destroyed. She didn't think she'd survive it happening again. Not with the Dantes. They meant too much to her.

"You gonna sign for this or are you gonna keep me waiting all day?"

Lucia jumped at the question and looked up. A man in a delivery uniform loomed above her, standing right up against her desk. She instantly recognized him. Henry. He'd dropped off envelopes and packages at least a half dozen times in the last month or so.

In a swift, unconscious move, she shoved her chair backward and jumped to her feet. "I'm sorry. I didn't see you there."

He held a clipboard with a letter-sized manilla envelope on top of it. Instead of handing it over, he stared at her, his gaze inching down her body in a way that made her queasy. "Lucia Benedict, right?"

More than anything she wanted to deny it. She gave a brief, reluctant nod. "You have something for me, Henry?"

Wrong question. *So* the wrong question. He grinned, though she couldn't detect an ounce of humor. "Yeah, I got something for you."

For an instant, she thought he planned to lunge at her. Maybe he would have if a deep, powerful voice didn't come from directly behind him. "Are you all right, Lucia?"

Ty Masterson stood just inside the doorway and relief poured through her at the sight of him. Henry's reaction was far different. His mud-brown eyes widened with a combination of anger and more than a hint of nervousness.

"Thanks for coming, Ty," she said, praying he'd read between the lines. "You're just the man I wanted to see."

Instantly, Ty crossed to her desk. Without asking, he relieved Henry of his clipboard and envelope and handed them to Lucia. "I assume you want this signed?"

Somehow, his maneuver managed to edge Henry toward the door. She didn't know if it was Ty's size or the sheer power of his personality, but within the space of a minute, he provided a powerful bulwark between Lucia and the deliveryman. She scrawled her signature on the clipboard and handed it to Ty who shoved it into Henry's hands and jerked his head in the direction of the door.

"We wouldn't want to hold you up."

"Yeah, right. Whatever," the man muttered before beating a hasty retreat.

Ty crossed to her side, his brows pulled together in concern. He started to reach for her, hesitating at the last moment. She stared at his hand, noting the size and power contained within the calloused palm, keenly aware of how well it matched the man.

"Are you okay? Did he hurt you?"

"I'm fine." The words escaped, low and soft and surprisingly calm. "He just unnerved me a bit. There was something about him. I don't know. Maybe I imagined it."

"It wasn't your imagination. I picked up on it, too. Always listen to your instincts."

Taking a deep breath, she lifted her gaze to his, taking in someone who couldn't be called handsome in the classic sense. Even so, the arrangement of his rugged, bronzed features was compelling, from his slashing cheekbones to the uncompromising set of his chin and jaw, to the wide, passionate mouth compressed in a firm, controlled line.

Most arresting of all were his bittersweet chocolate eyes, the expression buried within intense and brimming with secrets. They held her, examined her as though she were a strange puzzle he needed to solve. Desire slammed through her, the emotion both unexpected and unwanted. She fought it with every ounce of willpower, loath to believe after all of this time that The Inferno chose this moment and this man.

But deep down, she knew it had.

"It's safe to shake hands with me," he said gravely.

Suddenly aware he continued to stand in front of her with his hand out, Lucia took a deep breath and cautiously reached for it. "Of course. Sorry."

"Ty Masterson," he said, though she already knew.

"Lucia Benedict."

His fingers closed around hers and their palms melded. And that's all it took. She lost it, utterly and completely. With that single touch The Inferno whipped through her, a wildfire of desire combined with an itching burn centered where their palms joined, a trademark of the Dante "blessing."

She shuddered in reaction. If The Inferno truly were a blessing, why did it feel so much like she'd just been cursed? She struggled to conceal her reaction, desperately searching his expression for any sign he'd felt the enticing connection, as well, the spark leaping from her hand to his. Dantes and their mates always felt the burn the first time they touched. Did he? If so, he hid it behind an impressive mask of composure.

Had he felt it or not? She needed to find out, no matter how foolish it made her look. "What was that?" she asked.

"Excuse me?"

She squeezed his hand. "That. Can't you feel it? It's like static electricity."

Ty's eyes narrowed. "Sorry, did I shock you?"

"You're not feeling it?"

He released her hand and took a step back, folding his arms across his chest. "No."

"Are you sure?" she pressed. "A tingle. A . . . a sort of spark or burn or itch."

He didn't answer, just stared at her with those fathomless eyes, examining her with clear suspicion.

A desperate longing tore through her. "It figures. I should have known. I really should have."

"Known what?"

"That I'm broken." She flipped her hand over and glared at her palm, giving it a little shake in the hopes of . . . Of what? Kick-starting The Inferno? Reigniting the flame sufficiently for Ty to experience it? Jarring some internal connection so it would work? "Maybe my palm is broken. Maybe it's on the fritz. Or maybe mine only goes one way."

He tilted his head to one side. "You do realize I have no idea what you're talking about, don't you?"

"I'm talking about me being the first one in family history to have a one-way—" She broke off abruptly. *Inferno,* she'd almost said. She'd known this man for all of a minute and she'd almost confessed her relationship to the Dantes. What the *hell* was wrong with her?

"You were saying?" Ty prompted. "To have a one-way . . . ?"

"Never mind." She shook her head. "I'm sorry. I'm not making much sense, am I? How can I help you, Mr. Masterson?"

"Make it Ty." He hesitated, as though reconsidering his words. Then he shrugged. "I wondered if you'd be interested in having dinner with me."

"I'm not sure."

He lifted an eyebrow. "Is there something I can do or say to help you decide?"

She spoke without thought, an insane response leaping to her lips. "I'll agree to dinner if you kiss me first."

Chapter Two

Ty stared at the woman with open suspicion. Not that she noticed. She was too fixated on whatever insanity obsessed her. Figured. Bloody well figured. From the instant he'd first seen her, he'd been attracted. Hell, more than attracted. He'd been consumed with one overriding thought.

Take. The. Woman. Take her now. Make her his in every sense of the word.

Lucia stood, keeping the desk between them. A spicy-sweet fragrance drifted to him, one that somehow personified her. He drew it into his lungs, shocked by the unexpected primitive connection between her scent and his need for her. What the *hell* was wrong with him? Sure, he'd lusted after women before, but not like this. Never like this. Never in a way that struck at the very core of him, that turned him from a logical, controlled male into some sort of bestial throwback who lived, breathed, and acted on instinct alone.

He fought to control the visceral demand short-circuiting his intellect and reason. Fought harder to conceal his primal reaction to her. "Would you mind telling me what the hell is going on?"

She didn't back away from his abrupt question, and her composure impressed the hell out of him. He could sense her nervousness, but she contained it beautifully, running at direct odds to his own inability to regulate his response to her. "I'm sorry. I don't know why I said that."

He didn't cut her any slack. "Yes, you do. Something's wrong. What is it?"

She spoke so quietly, he had to lean forward to catch her words. "Have you ever had your illusions shattered?"

His mind flashed to his military service and the IED explosion that had taken out his entire team. Everyone, except him, though he still bore the scars from that hideous time, both internal and external. When he'd first joined up, he believed he could protect his team and country from all threats, only to discover in short order how far apart reality stood from dreams.

"When I served in the military, yes," he replied with impressive calm. "I imagine everyone has their illusions shattered at one point or another."

She left the safety of her desk and midday light from the nearby windows cut across her upturned face. God, she was beautiful, small and dainty in comparison to his massive size. High, sweeping cheekbones emphasized her delicate features, at odds with a mouth as full and ripe as a peach, one he wanted to lick and suck and eat. But it was her eyes that captured and held him.

They were such an unusual shade of teal, yet filled with an ancient pain that ran as deep as the sea and echoed its unpredictable, turbulent nature. She'd been scarred every bit as badly as he'd been and it brought out a fierce protectiveness. He'd never experienced the emotion on quite so personal a level. Nor had he ever allowed it to override the rational, logical part of him. Until now.

"What happened to you?" he whispered.

"I stopped believing."

He nodded in total understanding. Been there, done that. "I'm sorry."

She moistened her lips, hesitating, as though struggling to reach a decision. "Then something happened, something that made me wonder if I'd made a mistake. If maybe I just hadn't waited long enough. So, now I want to know whether I was right to give up, or if maybe there is something worth believing in."

"You've lost me."

"Maybe I can explain it a different way."

With those cryptic words, she stepped into his arms and rested her palms on his chest. She hesitated for a brief moment, watching to see if he'd reject her before sliding them upward and around his neck. He stiffened, tempted beyond measure to respond, but unsure of Lucia's motives. Then she tugged his head down and strung a series of kisses along his jawline.

He should resist. He should push her away and put an end to this insanity. Instead, he waited. His remoteness didn't deter her. He wasn't even sure she noticed. Or maybe the quickening of his body gave him away, the imperative insisting he mate their bodies in the most natural and basic way possible. Her movements became more assured, her fingers funneled into his hair and tightened just enough to hold him before she lifted on tiptoes and her mouth closed over his.

He fought to remain impassive, to allow the kiss, but not participate. That lasted an entire ten seconds. Maybe he'd have managed to survive long enough for her to give up, if it hadn't been for two things.

First came the tiny, breathless moan that seemed to slip from her mouth to his, filled with irresistible feminine pleasure. And second, she followed it with a hungry, nibbling bite that surprised him just enough for her to tease apart his lips and slip inside.

Tasting her was the final straw. He groaned in response, his arms closing around her. She tasted amazing, warm and honeyed. Her kiss deepened. A suggestion. A temptation. A promise of incandescent heat.

He took control, took her under in a tumbling wash of need. She shifted against him, her full breasts heavy against his chest. An image flashed through his mind. He could see her spread across satin sheets, arms holding him tight, her legs wrapped around him, taking him into her snug, moist sheath.

Yes, take her.

He cupped her breast, finding it nestled perfectly into his palm. Her nipple hardened, pressing against the silk of her dress. He eased the draped neckline aside, freeing her, and ran his thumb across the turgid peak. She felt amazing, her skin like velvet, smooth and supple and warm. She shifted closer, her belly soft against his erection.

He wanted to imprint himself on her. To stamp her with his possession in the most primitive way possible. He'd never experienced such basic and carnal thoughts before, but something about Lucia brought them to the fore.

The words came again, more insistent this time. *Take. The. Woman. Make her yours.*

He could barely think over the roar of the demand. It was as though she'd bewitched him, weaving tendrils of desire around and through him, the web of passion tightening with every passing moment. It filled him, overriding thought and intellect, consuming him.

He maneuvered her backward until they bumped up against her desk. She slid onto the surface and he stepped between her legs, her dress riding upward to accommodate him. A demand ripped through him, to tip her backward and splay her across the wooden surface. To rip the dress from her curves and worship every inch of her body.

He thrust his hand into her hair, the loosened curls winding around his fingers and clinging. The tidy knot at the nape of her neck surrendered to his gentle tug, unraveling and spilling down her back to just brush her hips. Dear God, he'd never seen anything more glorious. His hand fisted in the mass. Why did she hide this? Comb it into ruthless submission? The tumble of ringlets bounced, shivering in excitement at being loose and free. If he had his way, she'd always wear her hair loose.

He almost barked out the order, as though she were a junior officer under his command, but the words resounded in his head a split second before he spoke and he bit them back. One tiny splinter of sanity saved him, kept him from loosening a wealth of masculine aggression and demand on an innocent.

It didn't change how he felt. He'd never felt less civilized, never experienced such a crude imperative. But another part of him, a more rational part, spoke louder than the irrational. More than any other drive, his need to protect Lucia surpassed everything else. He'd listen to that voice. He had no other choice.

He dragged his mouth from her, nipping at the creamy sweep of her neck. Planting a lingering kiss at the sweet curve of her shoulder. Lower to the hard, tight pucker of breast. Another nip. And then another.

She moaned, shifting in his arms. "Ty, please." The soft cry drifted between them, sounding more like an order than a plea.

The words finally brought him to his senses. "This is insane." He kissed her to pull the sting from his words, passionately, then gently, before easing back. "We can't take this any further, sweetheart. Not here. Not now."

She reacted as though he'd plunged her into a bath of ice water. She surfaced with a gasp, shuddering within his hold. "What am I doing?"

He put a few inches between them so they barely touched and carefully straightened her clothing. "The same thing I am. Wondering what the hell just hit us."

For some reason, his comment caused her gaze to shy away from his, almost as though she knew precisely what had hit them. Not that it took much thought to figure out the reason.

Lust.

She was a beautiful woman and any man would be crazy to pass up the opportunity to hold her in his arms. Kiss her. Touch her. Make love to her. He'd just never before experienced such a swift, intense reaction to a woman, any woman. Never experienced their coming together so explosively within minutes of meeting.

"Should I assume that was a 'yes' to dinner?" he dared to joke.

To Ty's surprise, Lucia hesitated. She moistened her lips and he nearly groaned, tempted beyond measure to kiss her again. "No, that wasn't a yes." She paused a beat, flicking him a glance from beneath dark lashes, her eyes a flash of Caribbean ocean beauty. "That was a hell yes."

He grinned. "Should I pick you up?"

"Please. Seven."

"Casual," he countered.

"That sounds perfect. Why don't I give you my contact info?"

It only took a moment to exchange numbers and obtain her address. He should leave now. But he couldn't seem to convince his feet of that plan. Catching a tumble of curls in his fist, he drew her closer. "Until seven," he murmured.

And then he kissed her again, sinking into passionate warmth. As much as he wanted to deepen the embrace, he stopped himself. Barely. Drawing back, he released her. All the while, his inner voice snarled and complained.

Mine, it insisted. *She's mine.*

Lucia jumped in the shower the minute she hit her apartment, but refused to fuss over what she'd wear for her date with Ty. Casual, he'd said. Casual didn't require a lot of thought. It certainly didn't require trying on an endless number of outfits.

It did require a brief debate between jeans or a simple knit dress topped with a sweater. Black jeans and a dark bronze blouse won out. The blouse matched the mani/pedi she'd gotten in anticipation of the gala. Her one indulgence for the evening was a sky-high pair of black ankle boots that gave her some much-needed height. She kept her jewelry simple, as well, tucking away the diamond necklace Primo had given her and sticking to simple gold earrings.

That just left her hair and she pulled it back into a loose knot. Her hair had always been a mixed blessing. The curls were challenging to control and she'd often been tempted to go for a short cut. But Andrew had hacked off her hair, almost to the roots, during a particularly violent rage. After she'd left him, she'd grown her hair and kept it long ever since.

Right on the dot of seven, a firm knock sounded at her door. After checking the peephole, she unlocked and unbolted, trying not to appear as overwhelmed as she felt. Lord, but Ty was all male.

Although the word "gorgeous" leapt to mind, it lacked accuracy. Male models were gorgeous. Pretty boys were gorgeous. Ty didn't fit either of those categories. He towered over her, impossibly tall and broad, and exuding a toughness that left gorgeous and pretty in the dust. He also possessed a hardness about him that warned he didn't suffer fools gladly, yet an awareness of his own strength and the ability to keep it tightly reined.

Abruptly aware she'd been staring for a long minute, she swept her arm toward the inner sanctum of her apartment. "Would you like to come in?"

"You don't often invite people in, do you?"

She didn't pretend to misunderstand. "No."

"Nor do I."

She tilted her head to one side in consideration. "I've found that makes relationships difficult."

"Is that what you want? A relationship?"

She hesitated. Was the question a trap? "Why don't we just start with dinner and see how that goes."

He tilted his head to one side, mimicking her stance and attitude, though not in a mocking way. More in an assessing manner, similar to her own. "I can't quite figure you out," he admitted, his dark eyes narrowing in consideration. "One minute you kiss me, and the next you close all the shutters. Was the kiss an aberration?"

"Would it help if I admitted you're the first man I've kissed within a few minutes of meeting him?"

"I'm not sure. You asked—hell, you demanded—I kiss you before you'd agree to go out with me." A muscle jerked in his jaw. "Why?"

He deserved an honest answer. At least, as honest as possible, without mentioning The Inferno. He'd really think her crazy if she dared bring that up. Besides, he hadn't felt what she had. So, how did she explain the Dante curse if he hadn't experienced that bizarre burning when they'd first touched?

"I asked you to kiss me so I could see whether I'd imagined my reaction to you."

For some reason, her answer relaxed him. A smile lifted the corners of his mouth. "I assume you didn't imagine it." He didn't phrase it as a question.

Lucia grinned. "Nope."

She must have given him an acceptable answer. He gave an abrupt nod. "Come on. Let's go to dinner."

"So, that's a no to coming in?"

"Later. It's a later to coming in."

She lifted an eyebrow. "Depending on how dinner goes?"

"As you said, let's start with dinner and see how it goes from there."

Lucia nabbed her leather jacket from a rack by the door and slipped it on, then grabbed her phone and door key and tucked both into her pocket. "I'm ready."

"That's it? A phone and key?"

"Well, and a coat," she replied cheerfully. "My phone case has my credit cards and some cash. What more do I need?"

"I don't know." His brow crinkled. "Female stuff?"

"Ah, female stuff." She leaned in. "Well, just so you know, I have all my female stuff on me."

As though unable to help himself, his gaze swept over her, before returning to her face. "So you do."

"Not missing anything?"

"Not that I can see."

"That's a relief." She stepped over the threshold and closed and locked her door, checking it carefully. "I'm ready."

"I'm glad you take security so seriously."

Thoughts of Andrew flitted through her head, thoughts she firmly dismissed. He'd been gone for a full decade. She refused to let him steal any more of her life. "I take security very seriously." She linked her arm through his. "Where are we going?"

"Dinner."

She chuckled. "I assumed. *Where* are we going to dinner?"

"My place."

She hadn't expected that answer and her steps faltered. "Your place?"

At least her voice sounded even. She wished she could say the same for the rest of her. Maybe that kiss had been a mistake. She could understand if he'd misinterpreted it. She didn't entirely understand it herself.

But she'd had to know. Know if she'd really felt The Inferno when they'd first touched. Know if she experienced the instant connection and overwhelming desire when they kissed. Unfortunately, since she couldn't explain any of that to Ty, her motives were open to interpretation. Or rather, misinterpretation.

"I have a friend who's in town this week. Joe Milano is Seattle's premier chef and wanted to try out a new recipe. We're the guinea pigs."

She relaxed minutely. "Milano's on the Sound, right? I've heard of him. I think Gabe might have taken me to his restaurant when I lived in Seattle." She paused mid-step. "Just one thing I don't understand."

"What's that?"

"Why is he coming all the way to San Francisco to try out his new recipes on you?"

"Because I bribed him."

She couldn't help it. She laughed. "How do you know him?"

"I did a job for him."

"Really? What job?"

"A private job."

"Got it." She'd let that one pass, especially since she had a few secrets of her own. There was one thing she understood and understood well, and that was privacy. "Well, I'm looking forward to trying his recipe, even if you did have to bribe him."

To her surprise, Ty lived in a gorgeous Seacliff home overlooking the narrow section where the bay met the ocean. She immediately crossed to the bank of windows that spread across one entire wall of the living room. The November sun had set over two hours earlier and a sweep of lights glittered like fireflies across the Golden Gate Bridge and on out into the bay. She'd caught a few words of his conversation with Juice, before Primo had distracted her, but clearly not enough to explain all this. What in the world did he do for a living that enabled him to afford such an incredible place?

"This is gorgeous, Ty."

"Thanks. Make yourself at home. Can I get you something to drink?"

A stillness settled over him as he waited for her response. She found it intriguing. She'd observed the characteristic when they'd first met. Then, there had been a watchfulness, quiet but alert. Within the confines of his home, she noticed a slight difference. He relaxed. Settled, perhaps because his home was a safe place. She could totally relate.

"Perhaps a glass of wine?" she suggested.

He crossed to a mission-style liquor cabinet. A bottle of wine sat open and breathing. He poured two glasses of a deep, rich cabernet. He handed her one, then gently clinked his against hers. A sweet, high-pitched tone sounded, as though in celebration.

She sipped, the flavor exploding across her tongue. "Oh, this is amazing. Where is it from?"

"It's a Tuscan wine from one of the Dante vineyards. They're renowned for their cabs."

Before she could take a seat, a man appeared in the doorway. At a guess, he was their chef, Joe Milano. Now here was a gorgeous man, one who dripped charm. Not in an insincere way, but in a deeply masculine, wholly Italian manner.

"Welcome, welcome."

He greeted them as though he were the host and they the guests. Her mouth quirked upward. Perhaps that was how he saw them.

Ty stepped forward. "Lucia, this is Joe Milano, our cook."

Joe practically hyperventilated. "Cook?" he roared, his voice heavily laced with the accent of his homeland. Then catching Ty's grin, he slowly calmed and shook his finger. "Very funny, Ty Masterson. You should show more respect when you know I have full control over every bite you eat this evening."

Ty crossed to shake hands. "You're right, I should. I'd worry about what you might put in there to get even, but you care about food far too much to deliberately serve something you deemed less than perfect."

"That is the only thing that saves you," Joe retorted. He turned to Lucia. "You have a beautiful Italian name. Are you Italian?"

"Yes, both my parents were. Second generation."

His brows drew together and sympathy swept across his features. "Were? How sad."

In two swift strides he reached her side. Grasping her hands in his, he lifted them to his mouth and kissed first one, then the other. Perhaps if she hadn't been so familiar with Italians, she'd have thought the gesture affected. But after working for Primo, she'd discovered such gestures came as naturally to them as drawing breath.

"I will give you a fabulous reminder of your roots tonight, *cara*. By the time you finish you will be so pleased and relaxed that no sorrow could possibly find room inside." He swept a hand toward an archway at the opposite end of the living area. "When you are ready, have a seat in the dining room."

"Thank you for preparing our meal," she told him. "I hope Ty didn't put too much pressure on you."

"He threatened me with my very life."

Lucia inhaled sharply, only to release it at Joe's teasing grin. "Ah, you're one of those."

"Handsome? Brilliant? One of the world's best chefs? Why, yes. I am guilty of all of those." He winked, then left them with an elegant nod.

Lucia glanced at Ty and lifted her brows. "He's great. Really funny. Not to mention charming."

"Yeah, I suspect if he burped, it would come out rainbows and champagne bubbles," he said drily.

She grinned. "Come on, admit it. You wish you were Italian, too."

"I might be," he replied lightly. "My mother never told me much about my father."

Before Lucia could ask any questions, he caught her hand in his and drew her toward the dining room. Stepping into the intimate room, she caught her breath. The table had been beautifully decorated. Crystal sparkled. Fragile china sat on a lovely leaf placemat in fall colors. Silver gleamed beneath candlelight. And a low flower arrangement provided a lovely centerpiece featuring a cluster of roses in shades that complicated the placemats.

"Did you do this?"

"Joe did," he replied shortly.

"Got it." She slanted him a teasing glance. "It's very romantic."

"That was the idea."

He turned toward her, leveling her with the full power of his gaze. She considered Joe charming and sexy, but in a harmless way. At least, in her opinion. Ty hit another level altogether. Instead of charm, he radiated a powerful, masculine vibe. Sexy? Not even close. He exuded a fierce, smoldering passion that left sexy in the dust. Joe was harmless. Ty threatened to drag her under with just that single look.

She fought to breath normally, to hide the small hitching gasp those black, black eyes incited. If Joe weren't in the kitchen, she'd strip off her jeans and blouse and beg him to take her.

As though sensing her thoughts, he stepped closer. "Don't," he warned in a low voice. "Don't look at me like that or Joe will be eating dinner by himself."

"I can't help it," she whispered. "I can't explain why you affect me this way. You just do."

He jerked out a chair. "If you'll sit here, I'll get us more wine."

"Okay." She cleared her throat. "Just so you know, we haven't finished what you already poured."

His hands tightened on the chair and she half-expected the wood to splinter beneath his hold. "If you'll sit here, I'll get our wine and we can finish it. *Then* I'll pour more."

"Okay," she said again.

Lucia slid into the chair, keenly aware of him behind her. His heat surrounded her and his breath stirred her hair. She closed her eyes, longing flooding through her. His fingertips stroked her cheek and down her neck to the opening of her blouse. Inch by inch, he followed the downward vee, pausing just at the edge of her bra. He didn't move for a long moment. Aware she'd been holding her breath, it burst from her in a gasp, her breasts shuddering beneath that barely-there touch.

Her head tipped back against him in open surrender. "Ty . . ." His name slipped from her, filled with want.

He leaned down and took her mouth in a single, blistering kiss. Then he stepped back without a word, leaving her in a puddle of unfulfilled need. A moment later he returned with their wine. He set one glass in front of her, then took the seat at right angles to hers. She reached for her drink, praying her fingers didn't shake. To her relief, they remained rock-steady, which allowed her to lift the glass to her mouth for a sip that turned into a gulp. She noted he followed suit and hoped that long, desperate swallow indicated he'd been as affected by their kiss as she had.

Silence settled between them, though she didn't find it uncomfortable. More of a moment to regroup. Joe brought out an appetizer, *spiedini*, a dainty skewer holding a steak pinwheel encrusted with an herbed bread crumb, marinara, and a hint of sweet gorgonzola.

The chef remained to chat, though for the life of her, Lucia couldn't recall a word they exchanged. The *spiedini* left more of an impression, practically melting in the mouth and whetting her appetite for the next course, a cup of very delicate wedding soup.

"Are you ready for tomorrow?" Ty asked.

She winced. "I have to admit, I'm a nervous. At least I have a day off to prepare."

"Why are you nervous?"

It amused her how he cut right to the main question, always concise and to the point. The juxtaposition of his succinctness to Joe's lavish flattery was striking.

"I'm not a model. I'm not particularly outgoing," she confessed. "And I'm definitely not a saleswoman."

Ty nodded. "The Dantes don't expect you to be." He took her hand, stroking his thumb from her knuckles to her wrist. "The gala is high end, not a sales job. You're supposed to suggest a dream, create an illusion."

She took a sip of a second wine that Joe had paired with their soup, a fruity sauvignon blanc, and considered Ty's comment. "The men and women who attend will see me and imagine how they or their partners will look wearing something similar?"

"Exactly. Just be seen and mingle."

"Okay. I can do that." She grinned. "And when I start feeling uncomfortable, I'll chat with my bodyguard. Do you know who it is?"

"Juice."

"Not you?"

"You wouldn't be here if it were me." A strange expression settled over his face. A remoteness. "I never mix business and pleasure."

"That sounds ominous." She deliberately kept her tone light and easy. "Bad experience?"

"You could say that."

"I gather it isn't something you want to talk about?"

"No." He glanced away and then back again, amending his response. "Not yet."

"Okay. Fair enough. There's plenty in my own background that I'd rather not talk about. Maybe when we get to know each other better." She tilted her head to one side. "Or should I say if?"

To her delight, he didn't hesitate. "When. Definitely when."

The next hour passed in a total haze. Joe brought endless dishes, each course offering small, elegant portions, just enough to get a taste. Oftentimes, they each had a different option and he encouraged them to sample each other's dishes. A few questions followed, Joe quizzing them about various aspects of what they'd eaten. Though still exuding endless amounts of charm, when it came to food, she couldn't mistake his seriousness.

"I love trying your dishes," Lucia confessed. "You've done an incredible job. Do you ever get tired of cooking?"

"Never. I love experimenting. It . . . fulfills me on an almost spiritual level." He laughed. "I sound ridiculous, I know. But it is what I was meant to do. A job and aspiration I hope never ends. Does that make sense?"

"It makes perfect sense," Lucia replied.

The final course arrived, a frothy dessert in an unusual handblown forest green crystal flute, one side taller than the other. The higher edge looped over like a half-curled leaf to kiss the side of the glass. Long, small-bowled spoons allowed them to dig through the mousse all the way to the bottom of the flute to an airy raspberry sponge.

Replete, they took their coffee in the living room while Joe tidied the kitchen and the dining room table, before offering a brief farewell and departing.

Instantly, the atmosphere changed, grew charged and filled with a delicious tension. Oddly restless, Lucia crossed to the bank of windows and stared out at the sweep of lights crossing the bridge and dotting the bay.

Ty joined her after a moment, breaking the growing silence. His deep, dark voice slipped through the room, flowing over and through her. "Tell me what you want, Lucia."

She debated her options, but knew what she wanted. She'd known from the moment they first touched. "Please make love to me."

"Are you sure?"

She turned to face him. "Very sure."

His face remained in shadow, though his eyes gleamed in the darkness, filled with heat and undisguised desire. "I want you, too."

She didn't bother to play coy. She'd never liked that sort of deception in a relationship. Besides, she wasn't a virgin. She'd been married and divorced. And though she'd never been with anyone other than her ex-husband, she was far from an innocent.

"Where's your bedroom? I'd like to freshen up."

He jerked his head toward an archway. "Turn left."

She followed his directions and discovered a large, masculine bedroom decorated in earth tones. A single light lit the area, a soft shimmering glow emanating from his bedside table. His view matched that of the living room, offering another gorgeous view of the bridge and bay.

At one end she noticed another shadowy archway and discovered this one led to a huge master bath. She took her time freshening up, then debated her next move. Strip or leave that to him? Borrow a shirt or robe? She almost laughed aloud.

She hadn't really thought the evening through, hadn't brought anything with her in anticipation of spending the night. No female stuff. Shaking her head at her shortsightedness, she decided to return to the bedroom and allow events to unfold naturally. She entered the room to find Ty already there.

He was naked.

He was also painfully aroused.

Chapter Three

She'd never seen such a perfectly built man before. He was huge in every regard, his shoulders so wide she wondered if she could span them with both arms outspread. Muscles topped muscles along his biceps and down a chest lightly furred with dark hair, hair that darted downward in a sharp line, bumping across impressive abs, before surrounding his impressive erection. A worrisome scar carved a diagonal path across his chest and she wondered if the wound dated from his years in the military. At a more appropriate time, she'd ask.

Lucia forced her gaze back upward to meet Ty's. "I guess I should have stripped, too." She stepped closer, filled with a painful hunger that burned through her veins with each beat of her heart. "I did consider it."

"What stopped you?"

"I thought maybe you'd like to do it."

Oh, God. The comment hung between them like a hot demand. He instantly reacted, crossing to her side in two swift strides. She expected him to strip her without delay. He didn't. Instead, he stared down at her with an odd smile.

Ever so gently he cupped her face and took her mouth in a slow, leisurely kiss that threatened to melt the clothes right off of her. His tongue slid across the seam of her mouth, edging inwardly. And then he took her under in long, deep kisses. She shuddered within his hold, every part of her coming to life in urgent demand.

She pressed against him, her aching breasts tight against his chest, her arms equally tight about his neck, fingers tunneled deep into his hair. Desperate desire arrowed downward, settling in the very core of her. She needed him, needed him to remind her of what it meant to be a woman. It overrode every hesitation, every hideous memory of the only other times she'd been with a man.

He tugged her hair free, allowing it to surround them in a cloud of curls. "You are so beautiful. I've never met a woman I wanted as much as I want you."

"Never?" She pulled back slightly, searching his expression. Did he truly feel that way? Or was he feeding her a line?

He cupped her face again and looked directly at her. "Never."

"I shouldn't admit this, but I've never felt this way, either."

The palm of her right hand throbbed in reaction. A reminder from The Inferno. They still hadn't discussed the Dante curse. She debated bringing it up now, then decided against it. No. This was most definitely *not* the time. Especially, since it only seemed to go one way. She couldn't trust The Inferno. Refused to trust it.

He swept her under with another kiss and when she resurfaced again, she discovered he'd stripped away her shirt and bra. How had that happened? She'd never felt a thing.

He changed all of that in an instant, cupping her breasts and teasing the nipples into painfully hard peaks. His teeth closed over one and she cried out in sharp pleasure. "Ty! That feels so good."

"I promise, it'll feel better soon."

She didn't doubt that for a moment. He swept her into his arms as though she weighed nothing, catching her by surprise, and carried her to the bed. Tossing the covers toward the bottom of the bed, he set her on the mattress. For a long moment, he stood over her, an immense mountain of a man, simply staring down at her, as though memorizing this moment in time.

He planted one knee on the bed beside her and lifted a long strand of hair, winding the curls around his fingers. "I've never seen hair like this before. I think there's every color in there."

"Maybe not every color. But there are quite a few."

He lifted her leg to slip off her ankle boot, an instant later following suit with the other. Then he unbuckled her belt and lowered the zipper of her jeans. With infinite care, he slid her jeans and panties down her hips and legs in one slow move, uncovering her inch by inch.

His breath deepened. Thickened. Grew harsh and heavy. He reached for her, taking his time and giving her plenty of opportunity to end the moment if she chose. She didn't choose. She welcomed his touch, yearned for it. Longed to be touched with genuine passion and caring.

As though reading her mind, he accommodated. He ran his hand from shoulder to breast, waist to hip. Abdomen to the warm core of her.

"Tell me what you like."

"I don't know," she confessed.

For the first time, he drew back. "What do you mean?" A frown touched his brow. "Are you a virgin?"

She shook her head. "I was married." The less said about that, the better. "It didn't end well. He wasn't particularly interested in my pleasure." At all. In fact, he did everything possible to ensure she never experienced pleasure.

"Okay. I can work with that."

If she hadn't been half in love with him before, that one simple comment did it for her. He was seriously aroused. In her—admittedly limited—experience, men were more interested in taking care of their own desires, especially when in such obvious need.

He settled beside her and took her in his arms. "Tell me if I do anything you don't enjoy."

"I have a feeling I'll enjoy just about anything we do."

Despite his lips quirking upward, his expression remained serious. "Just let me know, though I suspect I'll pick up on it."

"Please," she whispered. "I want you to touch me."

Ty studied Lucia, blown away by how beautiful she was. Her hip-length hair spread in a halo around her head, thick, heavy ringlets that clung to him whenever he gathered them in his hands.

Her face was open, every emotion blazing across her elegant features. A flush swept across her cheeks, hinting at passion, and her teal eyes were dark and filled with mystery, a suggestion of longing peeking out.

Need rode him hard, and he fought to keep from revealing just how hard. Unwilling to alarm her, he considered his options, touching her with just his gaze. She didn't appear the least self-conscious, much to his relief. Definitely a good sign considering what she'd told him about her past.

For such a petite female, her curves were all woman with full, rose-tipped breasts, a narrow waist, rounded hips and slender thighs. A tidy strip of brown hair covered her mons, the curls even tighter than those on her head. She lay beside him, a visual feast awaiting a starving man.

He couldn't help wondering about her marriage, about her inexperience when it came to true passion. Had she never enjoyed being with a man before? God, he hoped not. That would be a damn shame. He didn't ask. Just like certain incidents in his past, he suspected that topic should remain off limits until they knew each other better.

She'd told him to touch her. Okay, then, he'd keep his touch light and easy. Slow. After all, they had all night.

He started with her face, using just his fingertips the way he had before dinner. He drifted from her eyebrows to her cheekbones to her jawline, and finally to the long, graceful sweep of her neck. And accompanying each gentle caress, he gave her a slow, deep kiss, drinking in her soft moans and sighs.

She lifted toward each stroke of his fingers, shifting restlessly. Cupping her breasts, he lowered his head to tease them with lips and tongue, and her back arched in response, pressing her body closer. She was so deliciously responsive, so unfettered in her reactions. He scraped her nipple with his teeth, releasing it long enough to gently pinch the hard bud.

"Ty!"

"Good or bad?"

She groaned. "Good. Too good. Not enough."

He gave each one another love pinch and followed it up by tracing a path downward to her abdomen. She had the softest skin he'd ever felt. Satin and silk and velvet all in one.

He slid lower, parting her legs wide in order to wedge his shoulders between her thighs.

He inhaled deeply, reveling in the scent of her passion. "Do you like this?" he asked. Gently he lapped at the core of her, parting her to reveal the deep pink inner layers. "And this?"

She shuddered in his hold. "I . . . I think so. I've never— I don't—"

"I can stop."

"No! No, don't stop."

He smiled against her, kissing the warm, sleek skin of her inner thigh. "Grab a pillow and hold on."

To his amusement, she fumbled for a pillow and buried her face in it, muffling her cries. He gave himself up to pure bliss, teasing the bundle of nerves peeking from its protective hood and sliding a finger deep into her passage. Her hips rocked upward and he added a second. She was tight, but her moist heat eased the way and he slowly pumped in and out. Curling his fingers slightly, he drew them repeatedly across the rough inner patch of her G-spot until she stiffened. With a muffled shriek she exploded in an intense climax.

He let her ride it out, then grabbed a condom and rolled it on. She instantly threw aside the pillow and wrapped her arms and legs around him. He took his time sheathing himself in her heat, pausing for an instant once he was fully seated. And then he moved, slowly and cautiously, giving her time to adjust to his girth.

They found their rhythm after a minute of experimentation, a brief fumble of give and take that elicited a breathless laugh. Her laughter turned to sighs of pleasure, then gasps of blatant need. Finally, she matched him, stroke for stroke, the breath heaving in her lungs. He drove her upward again, drove himself upward. Her cries filled his ears, urging him on. More than anything he wanted the moment to last forever. To hold them within this passionate bubble of time. But no matter how hard he tried, he couldn't.

With a cry, Lucia came and Ty followed her over, driving into her a final time, emptying until he had nothing left, locked within her.

"Don't leave me," she whispered, holding him tight. "Not yet."

Her words hit on some horrible, visceral level, tearing at him. They revealed such a heartrending vulnerability, spoke of a deep hurt that had never been excised.

He enclosed her in his arms, hugging her close. "I'm not going anywhere. I'm right here with you."

Ty woke in the early hours of the morning. At some point, he'd wrapped himself around Lucia, spooning her tight against him, enclosing her in arms and legs. Her head fit just beneath his chin, her hair twining around him as though taking root.

He smiled, surprised by the level of his contentment. Normally, he'd have held himself at a safe distance, but with Lucia, he didn't want to maintain that distance.

Mine.

The word echoed through his head again, a refrain he couldn't silence. Lucia murmured in her sleep, a small whimper of distress, and he gently turned her to face him. Instantly, her arms wrapped around him and she burrowed into his chest.

"You're okay," he whispered against his temple. "I've got you. I'll keep you safe."

He didn't know where the words came from or why the protective instinct hit so hard. He just knew he wouldn't allow any harm to come to her. Ever. She was his now.

For now, the bleak warning sounded.

He tried to thrust the cautionary voice aside. He'd learned he functioned best on his own, that lesson taking a bitter toll. He attempted to thrust the cautionary voice aside. When he didn't succeed, unease seized him.

He'd only met the woman in his arms hours ago. What did he know about her? They'd jumped into bed because desire had overridden all other considerations, their desperation for each other exceeding anything he'd ever experienced before. What happened when sanity returned? What happened if the flame burned hot and fast, then cooled to ashes?

He shook his head. No. He wouldn't worry about that now. He'd learned the hard way to take one day at a time. For now, he'd protect this woman with his life. Tomorrow? He'd let tomorrow take care of itself.

Soft morning light teased Lucia's face and she peeked through her lashes, struggling to figure out why everything looked so strange.

Then she remembered.

Warmth encased her. Male warmth. Delicious male warmth. She inhaled, drawing in Ty's unique masculine scent. If she could bottle it, she'd wear it every day for the rest of her life. She'd never fallen so hard, so fast.

The Inferno must be responsible. She couldn't think of any other reason why she'd jump into bed with a man she'd known for less than a day. She'd never done it before. Never even be tempted to have sex with a man who was little more than a stranger. Not after Andrew.

"Good morning." Ty's voice rumbled above her, rough with sleep.

She smiled against his chest. "Good morning."

"Tell me you're a coffee woman."

"I'm a coffee woman. Tell me you like good coffee."

"Oh, yeah."

Thank God, she mouthed. "Would you mind if I take a shower?"

He didn't miss a beat. "Would you mind if I join you?"

She shivered against him, the thought a delicious temptation. "I've never had sex in a shower before."

"I'm shocked, not to mention horrified," he teased, planting a kiss on top of her head. "You have no idea what you're missing."

Lucia peeked up at him and grinned. "I'd have an idea if you showed me."

"You're on."

"Then coffee?"

"Then coffee. You might have to drag me out of the shower and to the kitchen afterward."

"I'll tell you what . . . I'll drag you if you drag me."

"Deal."

Rolling out of bed, he shocked her by sweeping her into his arms and carrying her into the shower. He didn't release her until they stood in the middle of a marbled section of the bathroom, open to the rest of the room.

Ty pressed a series of buttons and an instant later, water rained down on them from multiple jets, some pulsating, others a hot, hard stream. Another press of a button and the jets eased to a soft mist that beaded on her skin like fairy kisses. In contrast, Ty took her mouth in deep, hungry ones, hurling her into instant arousal.

Then he backed her against the slick wall and cupped her bottom, lifting her so she could wrap her legs around his waist. In one swift thrust, he drove home.

"Oh, God, Ty. Yes!"

"Not too sore?"

She shook her head and buried her face against the curve of his neck. "Never. Even if I was, I wouldn't care."

"I'd care." His voice turned gritty with hunger. "I never want to do anything to hurt you."

And then he moved, pinning her against the wall with each frantic thrust. She tried to match his rhythm, but their position and the slickness of the marble made it almost impossible. Instead, she held on and let him take the lead, tightening her inner muscles in tempo with his thrusts, their movements building toward a frantic crescendo.

It didn't last long. It couldn't. For some reason their need had grown desperate, despite having made love just a few short hours ago. With a muffled scream, she came, clinging to him helplessly. He followed her over with a guttural shout. For long moments neither moved. Reluctantly, she released her grip on his waist and slid down his body. The water kicked on again, a warm, gentle flow that eased them back to reality.

He didn't speak, a characteristic she'd begun to accept. He simply ministered to her, filling his hands with bodywash and cleansing every inch of her body. She'd never had anyone take care of her like that before. Not ever. And yet, he did it so automatically, as though it were a natural part of his core personality. Then he made short work of scrubbing himself and that's when she noticed the slashing scars ripping across his back.

Oh, dear God! What had happened to him? Had he been in an accident? Or were these scars from his military days? He'd said he'd had his illusions shattered during his service. Was whatever had occurred to cause these scars responsible for that? She didn't dare ask. Every instinct warned her to let him bring it up at some point in the future.

When he finished rinsing, he gathered her close and kissed her with a tenderness that brought tears to her eyes. The more she knew him, the more he revealed himself through his comments and actions, and the more she tumbled, teetering on the brink of falling in love. How was that possible after such a short time? It made no sense, unless . . .

Unless The Inferno was real. Unless it had pointed her to the man who matched her needs better than any other. Isn't that what Gabe had discovered? And Primo and Nonna? And all of her half-brothers and cousins? Why did she resist what so many of her relatives had come to accept as reality? She shouldn't allow one bad experience to keep her from the dream. And yet, she shied from trusting. From believing. From attempting to walk through a door that might slam shut in her face at any moment.

"I'm afraid." The words escaped before she even realized they hovered on the tip of her tongue.

"Afraid of what's happening between us?"

Could he read her mind? "Yes."

"It's definitely strange."

He pulled her from the stall and wrapped a fluffy towel around her, dropping another on her head for her hair. Grabbing one for himself, he dried himself with brisk efficiency. Then he tackled her hair while she rubbed the moisture from her skin. Somehow, he knew to squeeze her hair and not rub it into a mass of tangles. Curls did not respond well to rubbing.

Securing his towel around his hips, he snagged his robe from the back of the door and tossed it to her. It smelled of him, a delicious combination of cedar and spice and some indefinable scent she couldn't quite describe other than: *Ty.*

"May I borrow a comb? It's going to take me a while to get my hair under control."

"Sure." He rummaged through a drawer in the bank of cabinets under the sink area. He held it out with a smile. "Coffee?"

"Definitely," she said, working at the nest of snarls her hair had turned into during the night.

He didn't bother to dress in more than a towel, just padded in the direction of the kitchen while she followed, finishing up one section of hair before moving on to the next. She hadn't seen the kitchen the previous evening while Joe cooked for them. Somehow, she doubted the chef would have allowed them to invade his domain, even if it belonged to Ty.

Lucia looked around, impressed by the state-of-the-art appliances and huge island workspace. "Do you cook?"

"Sort of."

She suppressed a smile. Working through the last of the snarls, she made fast work of braiding her hair. "I mean, do you *cook.*"

"Not like Joe."

"Well, no. I doubt many cook like Joe."

"And if you were to ask Joe, he'd say no one cooks like him."

She crossed to a small table set against a bow window and sat in one of the two chairs.

She tucked one leg under her. "You haven't answered my question."

He sighed. "I open cans. My stove is the microwave. It's not impressive, but it's eatable. Otherwise, takeout is my standard go-to."

"Okay." She hopped back up. "Why don't you work on coffee and I'll make us an omelet, assuming you have ingredients."

He pointed toward the refrigerator. "Help yourself. I'm going to throw some clothes on, if you don't mind. I just wanted to get the coffee started first."

"I don't mind at all."

It only took twenty minutes to throw together a hearty breakfast, preparing a veggie omelet for herself and one laden with meat for Ty. His appreciative smile told her she'd chosen well. She topped them both with roasted tomatoes and a dab of Fage yogurt she'd been surprised to discover in his refrigerator. Maybe Joe had left it behind.

Ty provided the coffee, a delicious Costa Rican roast, rich and full-bodied. Once again, they ate in companionable silence. Apparently, neither felt a need to fill the quiet with idle chitchat.

"Does this seem strange to you?" she asked, once replete.

"Us?" At her nod, he took a thoughtful sip of coffee. "Definitely. I wish I understood what the hell happened to spark such an intense reaction. Just chemistry, I guess."

Should she tell him? Gabe had once mentioned that their cousin, Gianna, hadn't fully explained The Inferno to her husband and he'd resented it. He'd felt as though all control had been stolen from him, not realizing that his wife had no control over The Inferno, either. That it wasn't something she'd done to him. It had happened all on its own, through some mysterious quality or ability of the Dante "curse." Or as some in the family preferred to consider it, the Dante "blessing."

"When we first touched, you said you didn't feel anything." She moistened her lips. "Were you just saying that?"

Ty's eyes narrowed. "I don't lie."

Lucia froze, something in that black gaze warning she treaded close to a line, one she better not cross. "Got it." She hesitated, unsure how to broach the subject of The Inferno, but driven to do so. "You prefer honesty, right?"

"I demand it."

"Do you know the Dantes well?"

"Not at all. I know Juice, their head of security."

That was a relief. She wouldn't have to confess her connection to the Dantes. Considering she hadn't told them about her existence, it seemed unfair to burden Ty with her secret. More importantly, she could explain about The Inferno without Ty figuring out her relationship to the jewelry icons.

"What if I told you there's an odd curse— or blessing, depending on how you look at it— that runs through my father's family." She spared him a swift look. He regarded her without expression which she suspected did not bode well for this conversation. From her limited experience with him, that usually meant he found the topic suspect. "I assume you don't believe in curses?"

He inclined his head. "Or blessings."

"Yeah, I'm not sure I do either." She glanced down at her right hand. "Except . . ."

"You experienced it?"

"Yes. With you."

He instantly made the connection. "This has to do with when we touched. Those odd questions you asked me."

She scratched at the itch centered in her right palm. "There's a reaction that happens when someone in my family touches the person they're meant to be with." She hesitated to use the term, "soul mate."

Somehow, she suspected he'd take to that with even less enthusiasm than a blessing or curse. "It's like a burning or spark."

"I'm guessing you felt it when we shook hands?"

She nodded. "Usually, the other person feels it, too."

"I didn't."

"I guess not." She hesitated, hoping against hope he'd confess to having felt something, anything, even if not the same thing she'd felt. "You didn't feel anything?"

He shoved his plate aside. "Lucia, I've answered that question. When we met, I felt an instant attraction." He managed a sardonic smile, though she sensed it was aimed at himself not her. "That should be obvious considering how things went from there."

She stared at the dregs of her coffee, as though she could find the answer to her questions hidden there. What did it mean that he hadn't felt anything? Had her palm misfired? Had she been mistaken? Had she wished it into existence?

He reached over and caught her hand in his, his thumb brushing across her palm. "Does it really matter, Lucia?" She shuddered beneath the stroking caress, The Inferno burning hotter, more fiercely. "Can't we just build a relationship on us, what's happening between us?"

"You don't understand."

"Then explain it to me."

"If we don't marry the person The Inferno chooses for us, the curse kicks in." The second the words left her mouth, she heard how ludicrous they sounded.

Apparently, Ty concurred. "That's ridiculous, honey."

"I know, I know." She shot to her feet and carried their plates to the sink. Turning, she leaned a hip against the edge and faced him. "When I say the words, even I have trouble believing them. It's just that every single person in my family has experienced The Inferno. I thought I was the only one who never would. Until . . ."

"Until you met me?"

"Yes," she whispered.

He considered her words for a moment, then shrugged. "Let's say you did. What does it matter? If you felt it, you felt it. Don't worry about how I experience things. You're attracted to me. I'm attracted to you. Let's just go with that."

Pain ripped through her. They were almost the exact same words Andrew had used to convince her to marry him. *I'm sure we felt The Inferno when we first touched. I definitely felt something. Not that it matters. You're attracted to me. I'm attracted to you. Let's just go with that.*

"I tried something similar with my ex. It ended badly." Lucia swallowed the acid gathering in her throat. "Very badly."

"I'm not your ex."

"But you're also, apparently, not my Inferno mate."

A stillness settled over him, a tension gathering, like a huge jungle cat preparing to pounce. "Does that mean we can't be together?"

If only she hadn't married Andrew. If only Ty had experienced some hint of The Inferno. And if only she could ask Primo's advice, explain what happened and find out why the reaction only went one way.

"I don't know how to answer that," she confessed.

"I think you just did."

He rose and gathered up the remaining dishes. She stepped aside to allow him access to the sink. "I guess we could just wait and see what happens."

The muscles along his back stiffened. "Lucia . . ." With a sigh, he turned to face her. He took a deep breath and slowly released it. "You're not the only one with a past. With a bad past."

"The scars on your chest and back?" she guessed, daring to mention them.

"On my back, yes. The one on my chest is from a train wreck when I was a child." She blinked. A train wreck? Before she could follow up on the comment, he continued. "I'm not sure we're on the same wavelength. I'm a logical, practical guy. I pretty much take the world the way I see it. I don't believe in curses or blessing or fairy tales. I've seen too many horrible things happen to believe in wishful thinking."

Tears gathered in her eyes. She didn't like the direction their conversation had taken. "What are saying?"

"I can't play the game you have in mind."

"I'm not playing a game," she insisted.

"Aren't you? Isn't The Inferno some form of make-believe game?"

She hesitated, driven to be honest with him. "I don't know. It isn't for the others in my family. And once upon a time, I thought it was real. Then I stopped believing until—" She waved a hand in his direction, struggling to keep her voice from breaking. "Until you."

"And if you decide I'm not your Inferno person? You'll just end our relationship?"

"No! Yes. I don't know."

"Well, I do. I can't go down that road."

"Wait." She stared in hurt disbelief. "Are you ending things?"

"I don't want to. But I don't think I can handle whichever turn your Inferno takes. I have a bad feeling it's gonna go south and I'll come out the loser."

"Please don't do this, Ty." She hated the desperate plea racing through her words. "Can't we just wait and see what happens?"

He crossed to her side and, as though unable to help himself, pulled her into his arms. "I want to. Please believe me. I'd love to see where this might go."

"I'd like that."

She could tell before he even replied that he hadn't changed his mind. "Listen, I think we probably should have taken things slower, though in all honesty, I can't seem to keep my hands off you. But I'm unwilling to compete with The Inferno."

She buried her face against his chest. "You don't have to."

His breath escaped his lungs in a sigh, stirring the curls on top of her head. "You know that's not true. As time goes on, you're going to question whether you've made a mistake. You're going to worry that you've chosen the wrong person because I didn't experience The Inferno like I should have. You're going to wonder if I'm not a repeat of your ex."

Oh, God. He wasn't wrong, though not about Andrew. His words echoed her own concerns. She fought against her tears, not wanting to use such a blatantly feminine weapon against him. "I don't want our relationship to end."

"Better it ends now before this goes any further. Let's just chalk up the past twenty-four hours to a special time together, but not something we should repeat. I'm something of a lone wolf, anyway, sweetheart. I don't do forever. I don't believe in it. Better we end it now before anyone gets hurt."

She squeezed her eyes shut. While part of her agreed with him, couldn't bring herself to trust in The Inferno or the possibility of soul mates, another part shrieked in warning. Begged her to claim him for all time. Warned that leaving would hurt far more than taking a chance. "Is there anything I can say to change your mind?" she asked.

He lifted her face to his and gave her a brief, tender kiss. "Not unless you decide The Inferno isn't real."

"I don't know whether it's real or not," she said with a passion that threatened to rip her apart. "I've spent over a decade denying its existence. I'd still be denying it if we hadn't shaken hands. But if you didn't feel it, too, then clearly, I'm imagining it."

"In that case, I hope you find the right guy. The one you're meant to be with. Because it's not me." His mouth twisted. "And I can't magically become that person."

It took every ounce of self-possession for Ty to escort Lucia home and maintain a respectable distance. All the while, he wanted to close her up in his bedroom and never let her leave.

He'd never experienced this level of response to any other woman, this primitive, primal demand. An inner voice insisted she belonged to him and no one else, and a chant ran incessantly through his head, threatening to drive him insane.

Mine. Mine. Mine!

It made no sense. It wasn't logical or reasonable or realistic. And yet, the chant continued with unremitting insistence.

Lucia maintained a brave façade, but he could tell it was just that. A façade. He'd hurt her. Badly. That hadn't been his intention, but everything he'd said to her in the kitchen had been the God's honest truth.

He refused to buy into her fantasy. Finding your soul mate with a single touch? Sure, it worked well for a fairy tale. But in real life? Not possible.

He exited the car, common courtesy so deeply entrenched, he couldn't do anything else. He took her hand in his, ignoring the small flinch she gave when his fingers settled against her palm. He considered leaning down and kissing her, then thought better of it. No point in torturing either of them.

She stared up at him, her heart in her eyes. The gorgeous teal color had darkened, turned turbulent, a storm in the making. And that gorgeous full mouth quivered ever so slightly, just about unmanning him.

"I'm sorry, Lucia," he said. "More sorry than I can express. I've hurt you and that was never my intention."

"You promised you wouldn't."

The words struck like a knife to the gut. "I know. I was wrong, even if it wasn't my intention. I'm sorry, honey."

She closed her eyes and drew in a deep breath. "I'm sorry, too. I probably hurt you, as well." Lifting her chin, she forced a smile to her mouth, one that didn't come close to touching her eyes. "I'll see you tonight. After that, we can go our separate ways."

He inclined his head. "Goodbye, Lucia Benedict."

She swallowed, her smile fading. "Goodbye, Ty Masterson."

She turned and entered her apartment. She never once looked back. He watched her the entire time. Watched those glorious curls give a cocky bounce and wave. Watched that incredible backside taunt him from beneath her tight black jeans. Watched those sexy mile-high half-boots rap out a reprimanding staccato as she marched up the steps leading to her apartment building.

Every part of him screamed to call her back. To apologize. To grovel. He yanked all those rebellious parts under tight control until she disappeared from view.

Mine.

Chapter Four

Le Premier, Nob Hill's exclusive, five-star hotel, hosted the Dante's gala. The place was packed to overflowing, despite it being five in the afternoon, suggesting that a sizeable portion of San Francisco had knocked off work early Friday evening in order to attend.

A buffet of appetizers and a bottomless wine bar tempted the attendees, but Lucia couldn't face either. She chose to stand beside her brother, waiting for Juice to come and collect her.

Ty hadn't arrived, yet. She didn't even have to look around to confirm it. Her newly acquired Spidey senses told her everything she needed to know. And with each passing moment, her tension grew.

As though reading her thoughts, her twin folded his arms across his chest. "I hear you went on a date with Ty Masterson."

She couldn't stop her shocked inhalation. Nor could she stop the words that escaped immediately afterward. "How could you possibly know—" She broke off, glaring at him in open suspicion. "You didn't know."

He grinned. "I didn't. Until now. I just noticed the way you two looked at each other when you first met." He spared a glance in his wife's direction. "It had a familiar feel to it."

Lucia's gaze slid away and she toyed with the diamond necklace from the New Beginnings line she'd agreed to model. The fire diamonds flashed with a smoldering brilliance, a painful echo of The Inferno. Leave it to the Dantes to own the only mines in the world to produce such unique and stunning gemstones, a fitting match for the family blessed—or cursed—with The Inferno.

Gabe watched her far too closely, his golden eyes, so similar to Primo's, narrowing. He signaled to a passing waiter and snagged two flutes of champagne, handing her one. "So, should we be toasting to new beginnings for both of us?"

"Why not? Cheers."

She touched her glass to his, the fine crystal singing out on a pure, cleansing note. She didn't dare tell him what happened between her and Ty. Not tonight. Not when it risked a confrontation.

Just the thought of him brought back that familiar awareness, a tingle that warned he'd arrived. Instantly, her palm itched and heat swept through her, filled with urgent want. If she turned a tiny bit to the left, she'd see him, tempting her to indulge in memories of their night of passion. She shifted to face right and pasted a bright, happy smile on her face.

"Where's Juice?" she asked. "Isn't he supposed to guard me tonight?"

"Escort," Gabe corrected. "You have more than ten million dollars' worth of precious stones dangling from various parts of you, brat. You need to be safeguarded in case someone decides to carry you off."

"When Primo asked me to fill in tonight, he neglected to warn me I'd be wearing anything approaching that much in gems," she forced herself to say, relieved to hear she sounded so calm. She didn't feel calm. Not even close. Bewitched, bothered, and bewildered, maybe. But nothing that could be called "calm." "Or that I'd need to be guarded. I didn't find out until yesterday."

"It probably never occurred to Primo to say anything," Gabe replied. "It's SOP."

It took a moment for his words to penetrate the sensual fog clouding her mind. "SOP."

"It means—"

"Standard Operating Procedure. Yes, Gabe, I know." The awareness grew more intense, creating a buzz of excitement. No doubt the champagne contributed to the feeling. She glanced down at her empty glass in surprise. She didn't remember drinking it all and yet clearly, she had. She struggled to pick up the thread of their conversation, latching onto it with something akin to desperation. "Most people are familiar with the term SOP. Since when did you start talking like someone out of a bad crime drama?"

Her brother grinned. "Since I was assigned temporary guard duty." He glanced over her shoulder. "Ah, here's my replacement now."

Recognition struck an instant before she turned to face Ty. Unfortunately, the warning didn't come soon enough to prevent her from revealing her dismay. "I thought Juice was my escort tonight."

Gabe leaned in and gave her cheek a quick kiss. "You're welcome," he whispered in her ear.

Oh, God. He thought he was doing her a favor. "I wish you hadn't," she whispered back, her voice far too uneven. Her brother jerked backward, his gaze flashing first to her and then to Ty. A spark of angry concern flickered there and she realized she'd once again spoken without thinking. "But I'm glad you did," she deliberately added with a teasing smile.

Reassured, he inclined his head in Ty's direction. "I'll leave you to it. Take good care of her. The Dantes are very protective of what they consider theirs."

Ty didn't reply. He simply folded his massive arms across his equally massive chest and waited until Gabe walked away. "Who is he?"

The words were calm, though a harshness underscored them. "Gabe Dante. You met him at yesterday's meeting."

"I remember." He waited a beat. "Who is he to *you?*"

She didn't dare admit their relationship, not now that he bore the name Dante. She swept her hand through the air in clear dismissal and the wedding and engagement rings she wore flashed fire. Primo had insisted she wear the set on her right hand, since he considered it bad luck to wear wedding rings on her left unless married.

"Does it matter who he is to me?"

She could tell he wanted to say more, but considering everything that had happened between them, as well as their final parting, she suspected he didn't quite know how to phrase it. His mouth tightened for an instant and then he shook his head. "I guess it doesn't."

"I'm sorry you got stuck with me tonight. I thought Juice had the assignment."

"It got changed." Ty's gaze scanned the gala, narrowing in on Gabe. Her brother stood with his wife, holding her close in a loving embrace. "He's married."

"Very."

"How does his wife feel about him kissing you? It's the second time I've seen him do it."

That caught her by surprise. "Second?"

He turned his head toward her, pinning her in place with his dark, dark eyes. "He kissed you right before the meeting yesterday. Why would he do that?"

"Again, it's none of your business."

"Are you lovers?"

The question hung between them for an endless moment.

What the hell was he thinking?

Ty wished he could take the words back. Wished it with every fiber of his being. And yet, the question burned through him, vicious and unrelenting. There was something between the two. He knew it as surely as he knew his own name. Were they acquaintances? Friends? *Old* friends? Ex-lovers?

Current lovers?

He regarded Lucia with open suspicion. Only one thing kept him from expressing any more unfound accusations. That damn voice in his head.

Mine.

The demand screamed through him, raw and unfettered. He struggled for his usual calm, to control his emotions and bury them deep. For some reason, when it came to Lucia Benedict, what he usually handled with ease became a hard-fought battle. She called to him on some level, tempted him like a mythological siren of old. And he responded, helpless to control the desire that swept through him.

Take. The. Woman.

He shook his head as though he could shake the incessant demand from his thoughts. It didn't help that he'd never seen a more beautiful woman. She wore a bronze sheath, almost Grecian in style, with one shoulder bared. A suitable look for a siren. Her gown clung to her curves, from generous breasts to a nipped-in waist, to gently rounded hips before falling in soft pleats to the floor. Her hair tumbled about her shoulders in heavy, loose curls and all he could think of was how he'd wrapped those curls around his fist as he drove into her.

Make her yours.

Not likely, not considering how Lucia glared at him. "I can't believe you just asked me whether Gabe and I are lovers, especially after last night. So, let me make this really easy for you. You ended things between us. That means you don't get to ask personal questions about me or my background or my past relationships. You sure as hell don't get to ask about Gabriel Dante or why he kissed me. Twice. Now if you'll excuse me."

She spun around, but before she took more than a single step, he stopped her with a light hand to her arm. "Where are we going?" He leaned on the word *we*. To his amusement, she swore beneath her breath. "You forgot, didn't you? Where you go, I go."

"Yes, I forgot," she admitted, blowing out a sigh. She stared out at the sea of people filling the ballroom, as though looking for an avenue of escape. "I wish I'd never agreed to this."

"That makes two of us."

The comment reminded him this was a job. He needed to remember that. Instantly, he snapped into professional mode, scanning the area. Off to one side, he saw the Dante family matriarch seated at a table. The instant his gaze landed on her, she beckoned to him.

"Mrs. Dante would like us to join her," he said to Lucia.

She seized on the suggestion like a lifeline. "I assume you have to come, too?"

"Everywhere you go, I go."

Her chin lifted and her eyes flashed like a storm-driven sea. "Not everywhere."

"No, not the ladies' room. But I will be stationed outside. And since there's only one ingress and egress . . ."

She took his words as the warning he'd intended. Oh, yeah. She didn't like that comment. Without a word, she spun around and made a beeline for the safety of the older woman.

Nonna Dante sat with all the regal assuredness of a queen. Even hovering on the cusp of eighty and bearing the wrinkles of a life long-lived, she retained a striking beauty.

She reminded him of someone, though he couldn't say who. He filed the thought away for future consideration. Her hazel gaze touched on Lucia before settling on him. Laughter dwelled there, as well as a deep, unsettling knowing. A wisdom and strength that combined happiness and pain in equal measures and chose to reflect the happiness, while accepting the pain.

She gestured for them to join her at the table and simply studied him for a long moment, before speaking. "You are Ty Masterson," she said, her voice as lyrical as Primo's. It also contained a richness, an underlying melody that spoke of warm, humid climes, as well as passion and laughter. "We have not met, I believe."

"No, Mrs. Dante. We haven't."

She waved his words aside. *"Ragazzo sciocco.* Call me Nonna, as everyone does."

He inclined his head. "Thank you. Nonna." He gave an amused grin. "Though I don't consider myself a foolish boy."

She lifted an elegant eyebrow. *"Parli italiano."* She didn't phrase it as a question.

"Sì. Ho imparato in militare."

"Eccellente." She offered her hand, holding his gaze with a challenging directness. "It is a pleasure to meet you, Ty Masterson."

He gained the distinct impression she was testing him. Without hesitation, he took her hand in his. The instant they touched, she closed her eyes, inhaling sharply. The next moment, she released him and settled back in her chair, her hand trembling ever so slightly. What the hell was that about?

For some reason, she avoided looking at him, turning to Lucia, instead. "How beautiful you look tonight." She smiled with genuine warmth. "Are you enjoying yourself?"

To Ty's surprise, Lucia shook her head, softening her response with a laugh. "Not really. Usually I love attending your galas. This time I'm incredibly nervous." She touched the diamond necklace encircling her neck. "I had no idea I'd be wearing such a valuable collection."

"Do not worry." Nonna glanced in his direction and he could have sworn she winked. "Ty will keep you safe."

"I'll protect her with my life."

Nonna's smile faded. "Yes, you will." Then she reached for Lucia with arthritic fingers. "Ty, would you please excuse us for a moment?"

Ty shot to his feet. "It was a pleasure to meet you, Nonna. You understand I can't go far."

"I do not wish you to go far. Just a few steps to the side. You will pretend not to hear our conversation, *ti dispiace?*"

"I don't mind at all."

She smiled at Lucia. "My dear child, you and I must speak alone for a moment, since I'm not sure we will be able to do so again in the future."

Lucia froze, her brows drawing together in consternation. "I don't understand."

"You will, my dear. In time." She tilted her head to one side, heavy white curls gathered in an elegant swirl at the nape of her slender neck. "Has my family told you about me?"

"Of course."

"No, sweet girl. Have they told you I have the eye?"

Lucia shook her head in confusion. "I'm sorry. The eye?"

She made a sweeping gesture. "I can tell things. See things. I sense who is pregnant. Whether it is a girl or boy. Events that will happen or will possibly happen." She paused before adding, "And I know about you."

Shock swept across Lucia's face. "What?"

"Do not pretend with me," Nonna chastised. She squeezed Lucia's hand. "I see you. I know you, just as I know what has happened to you."

To Ty's shock, tears glittered in Lucia's eyes, turning them to an incandescent shade of blue-green. "What should I do, Nonna?"

"Why do you ask such a foolish question?" Nonna reprimanded. "You know what it means, do you not?

Lucia nodded. "Yes."

"Then, you also know what you must do."

"You don't understand. I can't."

Nonna stiffened, drawing back. "You dare defy it?"

"I don't want to. It's just . . ." For some reason, she spared Ty a brief, pained glance, then looked away. Her voice dropped to a whisper, one he struggled to hear. It sounded like, "Mine is broken." Though that didn't make any sense to him.

Nonna chuckled. "Don't be ridiculous. Confess, child. You feel it."

"It's a one-way street," she murmured. "Has that ever happened before."

"Ah." Nonna sat back and considered. "No, it has never happened before. And it has not happened this time."

"I have it on excellent authority it has."

"Regardless of what you believe or have been told, you must not ignore it, Lucia. You know what happens when you defy it. You saw how it ruins lives."

To Ty's concern, a single tear splashed onto Lucia's cheek. "Please, don't," she begged.

Ty made a swift move toward the table, stopped only by the outrage in Nonna's fierce hazel eyes. Every part of him roared in demand that he sweep Lucia away from the old woman, and it called on every ounce of self-control to maintain his position. What the hell was going on?

"Decide and quickly. Time is against you." Nonna leaned in, her voice acquiring an unmistakable urgency. "If you wish to become a Dante, you *must* marry him."

Ty froze. Wait one damn minute. Somehow their conversation had taken a bizarre and unexpected turn. Marry him? Marry *who?* It was as though they spoke in a foreign language, one he'd only just started to learn and couldn't fully follow. Was this about Gabe Dante? Was the old woman encouraging Lucia to marry him? Dante already had a wife, as well as a newborn. Oh, *hell* no. That wasn't happening. Not on his watch.

"He'll never agree."

Nonna closed her eyes. "Then you will follow in the footsteps of others who have made the same mistake. May God guide your choice." She made the sign of the cross, suddenly looking every year her age. "If we don't speak again, please know I love you."

More tears rained down on her Lucia's cheeks. "You sound as though you're dying."

"One never knows when it is our time. I may have the eye, but even that door is closed to me. But I can sense—" She broke off and shook her head. "It is time for you to go. Consider what I have said. Consider carefully. You must marry him. It is the only request I will ever make of you, Lucia. You are the last holdout, and the one I worry about most. It will give me such hope for the future if you would do as I ask. Soon, child. I would live long enough to see it done."

"Yes, Nonna." Lucia hesitated, then leaned forward and kissed the old woman's cheek, whispering something.

"*Ti amo,*" he thought Nonna replied, but he might have misunderstood. The noise surrounding them made it difficult to be certain.

Without a word, Lucia slipped from her chair and darted across the room. He spared Nonna a swift, hard look, then followed, realizing his assignment had decided to escape onto the balcony of the ballroom, flashing million-dollar gemstones like a neon sign reading, "Come mug me."

He needed to find a way to get her back inside, even if it meant tossing her over his shoulder and forcing her to return. Two minutes. He'd give her two minutes to recover from her conversation with Nonna before he took control of the situation.

He made a quick scan of the balcony, relaxing minutely once he'd confirmed they were alone. Unfortunately, their solitude raised another problem, namely an overpowering desire, one that fogged his mind and attempted to overrun his thought process.

"Would you mind telling me what the hell is going on?"

Lucia crossed to the railing and wrapped her arms around her waist. "I grew up in Seattle. Did I tell you that last night?"

She spoke so quietly, he had to stand directly behind her to catch her words. A spicy-sweet fragrance drifted to him, one that personified her and reminded him of their night together. He drew it into his lungs, shocked by the visceral connection between her scent and his need for her.

"No, you didn't mention it."

"As much as I love Seattle, I have to admit there's something about San Francisco that's captured my heart. I wish I could stay here forever. But it would probably be better if I return home."

His reaction came in an instantaneous wave of shock. *No.* He almost said the word aloud, clamping down on it at the last minute. She shivered ever so slightly and with a muttered exclamation, Ty stripped off his tux jacket and draped it over her shoulders.

"Better?"

She snuggled into the depths and released a sigh of pleasure. "Thank you."

"What happened back there?" he asked roughly. "What did that old woman say that upset you so much?"

Lucia took several steps away from him. "Don't call Nonna that." She turned to face him. "She deserves respect."

"Not when she reduces you to tears."

"It wasn't deliberate. She just offered some home truths."

"Which were?"

A shaky smile touched her mouth and she lifted an eyebrow. "Didn't you follow any of it?"

"Maybe if she'd said it in Italian. I sure as hell didn't follow any of it in English." He planted his fists on his hips. "It sounded a lot like she told you to marry someone or else."

"She did."

He closed the distance between them, unaware of how intimidating it might appear until she held up a hand, stopping him in his tracks. "Gabe Dante?" he bit out. "Is that who she wants you to marry?"

He barely caught the hitch in her breath at his question. She eased backward and shadows wrapped around her, concealing her expression. Hiding most of her from him. All except her eyes, eyes that had haunted him from the moment he'd first seen her. A band of light cut across the upper half of her face, causing the blaze of blue-green to glitter like the gemstones that drenched her.

"What is going on between you two?" he demanded. "And don't tell me nothing. I'm a trained observer."

"Apparently not that well trained," she retorted.

Anger flared, burning with white-hot insistence. He fought to control it with only limited success. So much for professional detachment. "Just answer my question. What is he to you? Why does Nonna want you to marry him?"

Without a word she approached, two swift steps. The third pitched her into his arms and she wrapped them around his neck. Her mouth closed over his, the kiss devastating in its impact, making him forget everything. Forget their parting. Forget his past. Forget she was a job and he had a responsibility to protect her, not kiss her.

The words sparked to life, more insistent this time. *Take. The. Woman. Make her yours.*

A tidal wave of desire swamped him, taking him under and rolling him over and over until he no longer knew up from down. Only sensation remained. The need to lift her onto the cold stone balcony railing and shove her skirt up to her waist swept over him. To sink deep into her, pound into her, imprint himself on her so every man who saw her would know without any question or doubt that she belonged to him. That he belonged to her. That they were a mated couple and nothing and no one could come between them.

If anyone tried, Ty would destroy him.

Some small rational part of him whispered a warning, urged him to back away. To think. Think about . . .

What? What else was there beside this woman, this moment, and the blistering need burning through him?

The job. There was the job he'd been hired to do. He'd put his reputation and integrity on the line, promising to complete that job. And he'd never failed to honor his commitments before, no matter the personal cost.

And there was always a cost. An image of the child he'd almost failed to rescue flashed through his mind. He'd neglected to listen to his instincts then and he'd almost paid with his life. Now his instincts were screaming. This time he'd damn well listen. And it was that hideous memory which finally broke Lucia's hold over him.

Until he knew the deal between her and Gabe Dante, he refused to allow this to progress any further. Taking a deep breath, he ended the kiss. Wrapping his hands around her wrists, he eased her back, his grip firm and resolute, giving no quarter.

The chilly November air iced the gap between them, cooling the blistering heat. It took her a moment to gather herself, time in which he straightened her clothing, attempting to make her appear as untouched as possible, though one look at her face and anyone with an ounce of awareness would know what they'd been up to. She stared at him, an unmistakable question in her eyes. It almost killed him to answer her, but he had no other choice.

"I'm sorry, no," he whispered.

"You felt something. I know you did."

He inclined his head, lying through his teeth, but unwilling—or unable—to admit the truth. "I felt what any man would in a similar situation. Is that what you want? Another one-night stand? You know how the last one ended. I can accommodate you, though not until tonight's job is complete. I don't mix business with pleasure."

She jerked backward as though he'd slapped her. "That's *it?* That's all you felt when we kissed?"

Not even close. God help him, but he couldn't admit as much to her. Not until he'd had time to figure out what was happening to him. And why. Not to mention, what sort of relationship Lucia and Gabe shared. Didn't she get it? He was a loner. He wasn't capable of happily-ever-after and she had fairy tale endings written all over her.

"It was just a kiss," he said as gently as he could, feeling like the world's biggest bastard. "I'm not sure what more you want. Granted, it packs one hell of a punch. And if we hadn't already been down this road, we probably wouldn't still be standing here discussing it. That doesn't change the fact I was hired to do a job and I intend to accomplish that job. Then, if you're still interested, we can try this again in a more private venue."

"Got it."

Without another word, she stripped off his jacket and handed it to him. She'd turned into a remote goddess and he suspected tonight would end up being one of the toughest of his existence. He buried a sigh. What he didn't understand about women could fill volumes. Even so, he didn't go out of his way to hurt them and he sure as hell had hurt this one. She didn't deserve it, not after the night they'd shared.

"Lucia—"

She didn't respond, simply turned on her heel and headed toward the main ballroom. She opened the balcony door and disappeared inside. Ty scrubbed his hands across his face, feeling the unforgiving pull of scarred muscles along his back. He took a deep breath to help regain his calm and followed her. The instant he stepped into the ballroom, he realized he was in deep shit.

Lucia—not to mention her ten-plus million dollars' worth of diamonds—had disappeared.

Chapter Five

Fool! Idiot! What had gotten into her? How could she be so stupid?

Lucia slipped through the crowd making a beeline for one of several ladies' rooms in the corridors surrounding the ballroom. She chose the one located in the most secluded of the hallways.

She couldn't remember the last time she'd humiliated herself to this extent. Correction. Yes, she could. It had been with Andrew and she flinched from the memory. At least she hadn't lost all common sense and begged Ty to love her. Hot tears filled her eyes, threatening to overflow.

She pushed open the bathroom door, relieved beyond measure to discover it empty. For the first time that evening, luck swung in her direction. She crossed to the farthest mirror and set her evening bag on the counter. She studied herself in the mirror for an instant, distressed to see how easily her pain and disillusion could be read in her expression. She'd spent the past decade building barriers to prevent just that. With a single, passionate kiss, not to mention a stinging rejection, Ty had knocked down every last one of those barriers.

Time to regroup and fast. Lucia dropped her clutch containing her apartment key and phone on the counter and washed her hands, the special wedding set she wore flashing with brilliant colors.

Where before, she'd considered it indescribably beautiful, right now it seemed to mock her. The spectacular fire diamonds offered a forever love she'd never experience, echoing the fire of an Inferno that only went one way. As much as she loved these rings, they weren't the sort she'd have chosen for herself. She preferred something simpler.

Primo had once shown her photographs of his earlier designs, ones he'd created when he'd been intent on building Dantes into the international concern it had become. One set in particular had caught her interest, a lovely combination of wedding and engagement rings, that linked together, entwining love with commitment, symbolizing two separate parts becoming one. They didn't even appear to be two rings. Primo had shown her an updated version of the pair and the clever way they joined into a seamless whole.

"Before I met Nonna, I apprenticed with my *nonno's* cousin in Florence," Primo had explained. "Because my parents had never married, he refused to give me credit for my designs. Bad for business, he claimed. Our parting was not a good one and even after I immigrated to America, he remained angry for many years."

"Did you ever reconcile?"

Primo shook his head. "Sadly, we did not. I did reconcile with his grandson, a contemporary of mine who apprenticed at the same time I did. When his son became engaged, I offered to make their wedding set as a way to offer amends and reunite our two families."

"And they accepted?" she asked, curious. "They didn't want to make the rings themselves?"

He offered a "what can I say" sort of shrug, along with a broad, sheepish grin. "They did not own the only diamond mine in the world overflowing with fire diamonds."

"True, but that couldn't have been the only reason."

"No, it was not. They, too, wished to make amends, as well as acknowledge that the apprentice had surpassed the master. I called the rings Forever Dante, to remind us all that no matter how many miles separate us or how distant our connection on the family tree, we are Dantes, forever and always."

"What a lovely story. I'm so glad you were able to repair your differences with your family."

Dampness touched his golden eyes. "Sadly, the story did not end well. They and their young son were killed not many years later, after emigrating from Italy and becoming proud Americans."

She inhaled sharply. "Oh, no."

"That is why we must never waste the time we have been given. To gaze backward and wish 'if only' or regret not acting, that is a true sin against the gift of our lives."

Lucia stared at her image and fought against tears. Fine. She'd done what Primo advised. She'd acted. She'd thrown herself at Ty so she wouldn't look back with regret. And he'd refused her. Not once, but twice over the last two days. What more could she do? She couldn't make him love her, any more than she could force him to experience The Inferno.

So, how did she handle Nonna's demand? Considering what Ty had said, the two of them stood so far apart she didn't see any chances of finding some middle ground. He'd flat-out rejected her. Worse, he probably thought her crazy.

Well? Wouldn't she think the same thing if their positions were reversed? She frowned. Hadn't her brothers and cousins experienced the similar problem with their Inferno mates? How had they overcome their issues? How had they convinced their future partners that The Inferno existed?

Of course, it helped that both Dante and soul mate had felt the burn. Unfortunately, Ty hadn't. If it weren't for Nonna, she'd chalk the whole thing up to a misfire. To wishful thinking or imagination or desperation. But her grandmother insisted that she and Ty belonged together. *If you wish to become a Dante, you must marry him.* Lucia compressed her mouth, fighting the hurt that swept through her. They'd never made conditions like that on her brother, Gabe. Why her?

A hard pounding sounded at the door of the ladies' room. "Time to get back to the gala, Lucia."

She spared a swift glance toward the door and frowned, wondering how he'd managed to find her. Not that it mattered. As much as she hated to admit it, he was right, though if she could stay in here forever, she would. That didn't change one basic fact. Just like Ty, she'd been asked to model the New Beginnings collection, the most spectacular and costly one to date, and that's what she'd do. She might not have been hired for the job, but she'd agreed to do it, nonetheless.

Maybe she should also take the New Beginnings name to heart and stop her endless equivocation. When she returned to work on Monday, she'd have a heart-to-heart with Primo and confess her identity. She'd stop hovering on the outside, wishing she belonged, and walk through the door. Either they accepted her, welcomed her, came to love her as much as she loved them, or they wouldn't. But she'd never know until she tried.

Of course, that still left her problem with Ty. Maybe Primo could help with that, too. After washing her hands, she selected a cotton hand towel from the small woven basket centered on the counter. Dampening it with cold water, she touched the cloth to her temples and the side of her throat.

A muffled scream penetrated the quiet elegance of the ladies' room and Lucia's head swiveled toward the door. Had someone actually screamed? An instant later, more screams joined the first, along with loud explosive pops. Before she could move, the door burst inward and Ty sprinted into the room. Even more alarming, he held a huge, matte black pistol.

"We have to move. Now."

Endless questions bubbled through her and even though she desperately wanted to ask them, one look at his expression kept her silent. She snatched up her handbag and joined him by the door. He eased it open and checked the corridor that paralleled the ballroom. More, far louder pops reverberated nearby, coming from one end of the hallway. Ty grabbed her wrist and swept her in front of him and away from the screams and shouts.

She risked a single question, though deep down, she already knew the answer. She simply hoped against hope he'd give the response she really wanted to hear versus the truth. "Is that gunfire?"

"Yes."

She fought against the fear bubbling through her. It urged her to freeze. To hide. To run. Each emotion conflicted with the others. And then her thoughts flashed to her family and her fear took on a new, more overwhelming dimension.

Right before the end of the corridor, Ty paused. Two huge doors led into the far end of the ballroom, closest to the balcony. He tucked her tight against his back and edged open the closest door, taking a swift, assessing look around. The screams and shouts increased in volume.

"Listen to me, Lucia." He spoke low and fast. "We're going to enter the ballroom through this door. Keep down and remain in front of me. We're going to immediately exit onto the balcony. It's the reverse of the route you took to get to the ladies' room. There are steps on either side of the balcony. Get to the steps as quickly as you can. If for some reason I'm not still with you—"

"You mean, if you get shot," she interrupted, fighting to keep the panic from her voice.

"If for *any* reason, I'm not with you, do *not* return to the ballroom. Don't argue, just do what I tell you," he stressed. "Go down the stairs, into the hotel, and out the nearest exit. Do you understand?"

"The Dantes—"

"We can't help them right now. And my job is to keep you safe. That's what I'm going to do and that's what you're going to let me do." She opened her mouth to argue and he held up his hand, cutting her off. "Do you understand?"

This wasn't the time to argue, she realized. "Yes, I understand."

He nodded. "Move fast and stay low."

She longed to protest. Her brother was in there, her sister-in-law. Nonna and Primo! Oh, God. Everyone she had in the world was in that ballroom, dealing with whomever fired those guns. She fought against tears, fought against terror and shock.

Snagging her around the waist, Ty opened the door just enough for them to slip inside. Pulling her into a crouch, he raced toward the balcony door. She looked over her shoulder toward the chaos centered in the middle of the room.

Men wearing ski masks and holding guns swarmed systematically through the crowd of partygoers, shoving people indiscriminately to the ground. Shots continued to ring out and to her horror she realized that Nonna lay on the white marble floor in a circle of blood, Primo half on top of her. He had a head wound, one bleeding profusely. Neither were moving.

"Primo!" The cry escaped before she could stop it. "Nonna!"

Ty swore and yanked her harder toward the balcony door. And that's when she saw him. Gabe had his arms around Kat, holding her protectively. One of the gunmen seemed to be arguing with him.

For a split second, his gaze shifted, narrowing in on her. Time froze in that instant. And then the gunman turned his head, spotting her. With a laugh, he pulled the trigger of the gun he held and a shot rang out. Gabe jerked in reaction. Lucia jerked, as well, screaming in anguish, her knees giving out on her.

As though in slow-motion, Gabe fell, sprawling to the floor, a harsh black figure against a sea of brilliant white. With a cry, Kat dropped down beside him.

The gunman started toward her, his voice echoing across the chaotic ballroom. "Lucia! Just the one I wanted."

Beside her, Ty swore, the word harsh and bitter. He yanked her to her feet and tossed her over his shoulder. Then he burst through the door to the balcony at a dead run. Lucia could only hang on, aware on some level she was sobbing and calling for Gabe. She retained only flashes of memory of Ty pounding down the steps and rushing out of the hotel. She finally snapped back into focus when he dropped her to her feet on the sidewalk outside of Le Premier, the chilly November air waking her to her surroundings.

Sirens sounded nearby, approaching far too slowly, their progress impeded by the remnants of rush hour crowding the busy Nob Hill streets. Ty's gun had disappeared, no doubt tucked away where he could get his hands on it quickly, if necessary. He hustled her down the steep hill on California St. in the direction of China Town, helping her when her heels caused her to stumble, when shock had her legs threatening to give out on her. A trolley car rumbled to a stop at Powell, and he tossed her into one of the seats along the outside and stood directly in front of her on the running board, his massive height and width totally blocking her from view.

Neither spoke. She couldn't gather her wits sufficiently to ask the endless questions ricocheting around inside her head, not when her fear for Gabe and Primo and Nonna edged out every other thought and consideration. She shivered, the cold creeping deep into her bones. She'd forgotten her coat at the hotel. The errant thought drifted past, like a scattered leaf blown helter-skelter before a frigid autumn wind.

Were they dying? Were they dead?

Tears pooled in her eyes and slid silently down her cheeks. Nonna had known. She'd known something was coming. Something bad. That her life would soon end. An endless litany of "if onlys" bombarded her.

If only she'd told the Dantes her true identity. If only she hadn't been so afraid. If only she'd hugged Primo. If only she'd told Gabe she loved him one more time.

If only.

The cable car jerked to a stop and Ty stepped off the running board, offering his hand to help her down. "We need to get to your place so you can change and grab some things," Ty said.

Lucia stared at him blankly. "Things?"

"They knew you, Lucia. The gunmen knew you. Either you're one of them—"

Her mouth fell open in shock. *"What?"*

He nodded as though she'd confirmed something. "Or the gunmen were specifically targeting you. Until we find out which, we need a safe place to stay while the police sort this out. That's definitely not your place, though we probably have a few minutes to grab some essentials before anyone thinks to track you down there."

"Oh." For some reason, she couldn't get her brain to work. Everything felt muddled and confused. Out of focus and distant. She glanced around, as though expecting her apartment key to magically appear. When it didn't, she offered Ty a helpless look. "My handbag is gone. My key is in it."

"Okay. We'll go to my place." He glanced around, his mouth compressing. "Give me your jewelry. It's not safe to walk around flashing that much bling. We're just asking for trouble."

Without a word, she stripped off the necklace and earrings, followed by the bracelet and wedding rings. She dumped the lot into his hand. He dropped them into his jacket pocket and then lifted his hand toward a cruising cab.

"Don't say anything until we're inside my house, got it?"

She didn't bother to protest. Right now, she found it easier to do as instructed without argument. For some reason, she couldn't organize her thoughts well enough to string a coherent sentence together, let alone the brain cells necessary for any sort of dispute.

The ride took far too long and gave her far too much time to think and speculate and worry. She also couldn't seem to get warm, hard shudders ripping through her.

Ty stripped off his tux jacket and, once again, wrapped it around her. "It's shock," he murmured in a voice too low for the driver to hear.

He told her not to speak until they reached his place, but she had to ask. "Can we call and get an update once we arrive?"

"Definitely."

"Thanks."

Finally, the cab pulled up outside Ty's house. He paid the driver and escorted her inside. Without a word, he steered her toward his bedroom and straight through to the bathroom. Without delay, he turned the water in the shower on high.

"Strip and get in. A hot shower should warm you up. I'll fix coffee and make some calls."

She wanted to refuse, but she shivered so hard, she didn't see any point in arguing. "I won't be long," she said through chattering teeth.

"I should have an update by the time you're done."

Even removing her clothing became an almost impossible task, her hands refusing to cooperate with her brain. She let everything drop in a haphazard pile, the gorgeous spill of bronze against the pale stone tiles reminding her all too vividly of the spill of dark red blood against the ballroom's white marble floor.

With a shudder, she entered the shower, the hot spray relaxing muscles she didn't realize she'd clenched, and warming her to the point that the shaking finally subsided. Worry over her brother superseded her own needs, however, so she didn't linger. After drying off, she snatched up Ty's robe from the back of the door, fighting against a twinge of déjà vu. Knotting the sash, she made a beeline for the living room.

"Okay, thanks Juice. We're going to stay here for now, but I'm concerned that we're fairly easy to find. Also, Lucia's missing her purse. Her apartment key and cell are in there. Ask around and see if anyone found it. If not, the police might want to stake out her apartment in case someone makes a run at her there." He fell silent for a moment, listening. "Huh. Okay, I might take them up on that offer."

Ty turned to face Lucia, his eyes narrowing with unmistakable heat at the sight of her. He might pretend indifference, but apparently that's all it was. A pretense. Despite her fear and panic, it gave her some measure of hope.

"I appreciate it. Let's touch bases in an hour," he said, concluding the call. Before she could even ask, he offered immediate reassurance, rattling off the facts in a brisk, calm manner. "I'm guessing Gabe is probably your primary concern. He was shot. It didn't hit anything vital. Fortunately, the gunman has piss-poor aim. It's a through and through to the shoulder. He'll spend a night in the hospital."

She didn't bother to deny her first thoughts were of her brother. Relief hit hard enough that she sank onto the edge of the couch. It took a moment to gather herself sufficiently to speak. "Primo? Nonna?"

He hesitated. "Primo received a superficial wound to the head."

Alarm shot through her. "And Nonna?"

"Not good. She's in critical condition."

Lucia covered her mouth, fighting tears. "She knew. She knew something would happen."

He didn't respond to her comment. Instead, he added a generous shot of bourbon to the coffee sitting on the table in front of the couch. Harsh lines bracketed Ty's mouth and tension poured off him. He handed her one of the mugs and took the other for himself.

"We need to talk."

"Could I call Gabe, first?" Instantly, Ty's expression tightened and she hastened to explain. "I . . . I need to let him know I'm okay."

To her consternation, he shook his head before she even finished speaking and she fought to control the hectic mix of emotions sweeping through her. Fear tripped over desperation, the remnants of shock combining with the impetus to act, all of which spiraled through her, winding her tighter and tighter.

"I can't let you speak to him until after we talk. Right now, he's getting patched up. Juice will tell him you're safe and with me."

One look warned of the futility of arguing. She'd left her cell phone in her handbag and couldn't remember what had happened to either one, any more than she could recall where or when she might have lost them. The bathroom? The ballroom? The balcony or street? All of those were distinct possibilities.

Bottom line, she wouldn't have access to a phone until he allowed it. She curled into a tight ball and cradled her coffee, taking a tiny sip. The bourbon burned a path downward, finishing the job the shower had started, sending a delicious heat racing through her.

Taking a deep breath, she decided to jump in with both feet, fighting to keep her voice even and free of the emotions surging through her. "You said you thought I was involved in the attack on the gala."

He took a seat on the opposite end of the couch, turning to face her. "It's one possibility, considering the gunman knew you." He held up a hand at her incipient protest. "I've mixed business and pleasure in the past and ended up betrayed. Pleasure turned into a setup that almost cost a young boy his life." Dangerous shadows burned within his gaze. "Convince me you're not a repeat of pleasure turning into a setup that's going to cost lives."

"I'd never do anything to hurt the Dantes," she insisted. "I'd never put their lives at risk. Ever."

"Why? What are the Dantes to you, Lucia? I'm not stupid." He fixed hard and determined eyes on her. "It's more than an employee/employer relationship. Explain what's going on."

She steeled herself. Time to come clean. She'd hidden her identity long enough. "They're my family," she confessed. "Gabe is my brother, not my lover. My twin brother."

She'd shocked him. Honest to God shocked him. She'd find it amusing, if the circumstances weren't so serious. "Your *brother?*"

"Primo and Nonna are my grandparents."

Ty took a moment to analyze her words, then shook his head. "Primo called you his executive assistant, not his granddaughter. None of the Dantes said anything about the relationship."

"Because they don't know." She buried her nose in her coffee cup, taking a deeper sip, needing the hit of bourbon every bit as much as the caffeine. "It's a long, sordid story."

"Let me guess. You and Gabe are illegitimate."

She nodded, impressed by his insight. "You met Sev, right?"

"Dantes CEO."

She nodded. "He and his three brothers are my half-siblings. Sev's father and my mother had an affair. None of the Dantes knew about it until recently. And when they found out, we never told them there were two of us. Only Gabe."

"Why?"

She shrugged. "Once upon a time, it's all I dreamed of. Now, I'm not certain I want to be a Dante, anymore. Circumstances change. I've changed."

He gave a slow nod. "Understandable you'd hesitate to chase an unfulfilled dream from your youth once you reached adulthood.

Since the Dantes are unaware of your identity, I assume your father never acknowledged you?"

"No." She hated opening the old wounds. Maybe she never would have if she didn't consider it imperative he understand why she'd never betray the Dantes. "My father promised he'd leave his wife for my mother. Maybe he would have." She shrugged. "Hard to say at this late juncture if it ever would have happened."

"Why not?"

"He was killed in a sailing accident along with Sev's mother not long after he'd made the promise, so I guess we can never be one hundred percent certain. The cynical part of me says he wouldn't have left her."

"And you went to work for Primo in order to get to know the family better without them being aware of the relationship?"

"Exactly." She leaned toward him. "I'm not involved in this attack, regardless of what you might think. I couldn't do such a thing. I wouldn't put my entire family at risk. It's unthinkable."

His expression remained implacable, his thoughts hidden from her. "Or maybe you helped plan the robbery in order to get even with them for what your father did to you and your brother. The woman who betrayed me was the boy's aunt. And yet she still attempted to use me to funnel info to the kidnappers for a share of the ransom money."

Her breath hitched and her eyes widened in horrified disbelief. "You think I'd do such a thing when my brother and sister-in-law were in the room? You can't seriously believe that?"

"No, I don't." Ty paused a beat before replying. "But the police might consider that a possible motive. At the very least, they'll give it serious consideration."

"I am not involved," she repeated flatly.

"But you knew the man who shot your brother. Or he knows you," Ty pressed. "He called you by name. That means there's a connection there."

She shook her head throughout his recital. "No. No. *No!* I have no idea who he is or how he knows me. I'd never be involved with someone capable of what he's done."

"But there's a link," Ty insisted in uncompromising tones. "You might not recall how right now, but when the police finally identify him, I guarantee. You'll have had contact with him in some capacity at some point."

She didn't bother arguing. No matter how hard she fought the concept, his words made a hideous sort of sense. "So, now what?"

"For now, we sit tight. At some point, we need to speak to the police. Before that happens, I want to make sure you're safe, and that means a secure location."

She glanced around. "Isn't this a secure location?"

"It's as safe as I can make it. But a determined team, like the one that attacked the gala? They could breach the place without too much trouble." He finished his coffee and set the cup to one side. "Juice is looking into a place for us to stay, one that isn't associated with either one of us. You're sure no one but Gabe knows you're a Dante?"

She fought to get the words out. "Nonna knows."

His voice gentled. "Nonna isn't currently a factor."

"I should have told them." She bowed her head, the level of regret sweeping through her crippling in its intensity. "I should have told them who I really was."

"It wouldn't have changed anything."

Her head jerked back up. "Not tonight, I realize that. But they could have been my grandparents during this past year, instead of my employers." She set her cup aside. "I'd like to call Gabe now."

Without a word, he passed her his cell phone. Gabe answered on the first ring. "Masterson?"

To Lucia's horror, a huge, gut-wrenching sob choked her. It took her three tries to get her brother's name out. "Gabe? Are you okay?"

"Oh, thank God. You have no idea how relieved I am to hear your voice. Juice said you weren't injured, but—" He ended the comment abruptly. "Well, no point in going there."

"How are you?" Her voice rose, despite her attempt to control it. "I saw you get shot."

"I'm fine, Lucia. Fine. A bit of pain." He broke off with a rough laugh. "Okay, a lot of pain. But I'm okay. You?"

"Ty got me out of there right after you were shot."

"Lucia . . ." Gabe's voice dropped to a whisper. "The police are here."

"Why are you whispering?"

"He knows you, honey. Somehow the gunman knows you. He was asking about you. He even knew we were related and demanded

I take him to you. Then you came into the ballroom. The minute he saw you, that's when he shot me. Lucia, he recognized you."

Her fingers trembled and she tightened her grip on the phone. Ty slipped it from her hand and put the phone on speaker. "This is Ty Masterson. You're on speaker. I'm here with your sister. Repeat what you just said."

"The gunman knows Lucia by sight and by name, as well as my connection to her. He shot me right after spotting her."

"You think he shot you *because* Lucia saw the two of you together?" Ty clarified.

Gabe spoke fast and low. "I think he shot me because it would hurt her. He said, 'Now you'll know how it feels.' You have to keep her safe, Masterson. All but one of them got away."

"The one who shot you escaped?" Urgency underscored the question.

"Yes. And the one they have in custody is in critical condition. They're not going to get anything out of him for a while."

"How's Nonna?" Lucia interrupted.

"It's bad." He paused and a harsh sigh issued through the line. "They don't think she's going to make it."

"Oh, no." Lucia covered her mouth with her hand. "I have to see her."

"No. If you come to the hospital, the police will take you in. Based on their questions, they think you're involved somehow. If not directly complicit, then connected in some capacity."

Ty shot her an "I told you so" look. "I'll keep her away."

"But what about Nonna?" Lucia protested.

"She's unconscious. There's nothing you can do for her. Listen, I have to go. Masterson?"

"Still here."

"Keep her safe."

"I will."

The line went dead and Lucia shot to her feet, pacing from the couch to the bank of windows overlooking the bay. "I don't understand any of this."

"And yet, somehow you're at the heart of it." His phone rang and, after checking the caller ID, he answered. "Is it okay to put you on speaker, Juice?"

Apparently, he agreed because his deep voice filled the room an instant later. "I've arranged for a rental car to be dropped off first thing tomorrow. You'll find a suitcase for Lucia with clothes and toiletries. I'll send you the address for the Dantes' lake house. It's about a three-hour drive. The caretakers will open up the main house and have it fully stocked for you."

"Okay, thanks."

"Wait. What's going on?" Lucia interrupted.

"Sev has arranged for the two of you to get out of town until we have more information on who attacked the gala and why, other than the obvious," Juice filled her in. "We want to get you to a safe location until we figure out more."

"He . . . he doesn't think I'm involved?" she asked unevenly

"Hell, no." His instantaneous reply had her closing her eyes in relief. "None of us believes that for a minute."

"Even though one of the gunmen recognized me?"

"Even though."

She buried her face in her hands and turned away, her throat closing over. She vaguely heard Juice and Ty conversing, though she didn't catch the actual words. Only one fact penetrated. Her family believed in her. Trusted her. Despite being unaware of her connection to them, they still supported her. Why in the world had she held herself at a distance from them? She was a fool. A total and utter fool.

Ty's heavy hands settled on her shoulder, turning her into his comforting hold. She nestled against him, losing herself in his warm embrace. "It's going to be okay, Lucia," he murmured close to her ear. "The police will figure it out, I promise. They'll catch whoever did this."

"And Nonna?"

"We take it hour by hour, one day at a time."

"She knew." Lucia lifted her head, struggling to see Ty clearly through tear-blurred eyes. "She knew something was going to happen."

He didn't argue. He also didn't agree. "We need to get some sleep."

She released a short, harsh laugh. "Right. I'm sure that'll happen."

"We have an early start in the morning. We should rest while we can."

"I can rest, but I doubt I'll sleep."

"You will after another shot of bourbon." Releasing her, he crossed to a liquor cabinet and poured her a drink. Crossing to her side, he wrapped her hands around the crystal highball glass. "Drink."

She wanted to protest. But one look at his expression had her lifting the glass to her lips and tossing back the smoky-sweet liquor. It scalded the back of her throat, but she swallowed it down, her eyes watering.

"What happened to the boy?" she asked.

"I rescued him."

But not without incident. The hard brevity of his reply to her that much. "And the aunt?"

"In jail."

"She's why you don't mix business and pleasure?"

He inclined his head. "She's the reason." Lucia could tell she wouldn't get more out of him about it. Sure enough, he changed the subject. "Would you be more comfortable sleeping in my robe or a T-shirt?"

The question caught her off guard and she took another gulp of bourbon, the alcohol a harsh burn from tongue to belly. "T-shirt." The word escaped in a strangled gasp and she tried again. "T-shirt."

"Alone or with company?"

She didn't hesitate. "Company."

He inclined his head in the direction of the bedroom. "Let's go."

It definitely felt like déjà vu all over again. She led the way, standing awkwardly in the middle of the room while he removed a shirt from his dresser and tossed it in her direction. "You already know where I keep the spare toiletries."

She escaped into the bathroom, only then realizing she'd left her designer gown in a heap on the tile floor. She picked it up and returned to the bedroom to hang it up, stumbling to a halt. Ty had stripped off his tux and stood with his back to her.

He was completely naked. Again.

Chapter Six

Her sharp inhalation alerted him to her return and he spun around to face her. Her gaze dipped downward, freezing on his erection. What to do, what to do? Not that it took a huge amount of thought. She either turned from him or she surrendered to him.

Without a word, she allowed the gown she held to tumble to the floor once again and untied her robe. Snatching a swift breath, she let it slide off her shoulders, waiting to see if he'd reject her again.

He didn't.

In two swift strides, he reached her side and swept her into his arms. He carried her to the bed and they sank to the mattress, entwined in a desperate jumble of arms and legs. She needed this. Right now, she needed to have life reaffirmed, to have just one moment out of time to feel love and be loved.

"Are you sure?" she asked.

"Positive." He fought to find a condom and put it on.

"Even though I'm your assignment and you don't mix work and pleasure?"

He didn't hesitate. "Even though. Apparently, I haven't learned a damn thing from my past."

She decided not to go there. "And even though you think I'm bat-shit crazy to believe in The Inferno?"

His lips twitched into a slow grin. "Even though."

He lowered his head to take her mouth in a deep, thorough kiss. In one swift move he joined them, surging inward with a single aggressive thrust. Then he froze, allowing them both to savor the moment. He lifted her arms above her head and interlocked her fingers with his, palm against palm.

The burn of The Inferno flooded through her, linking them as inexorably as Ty had linked their bodies. It burrowed deep, a wildfire of scorching need. "Why doesn't your palm burn, too?" The words escaped in a groaning sigh.

"Every part of me burns." He lowered his head to kiss the sensitive curve where neck joined shoulder. "You're all around me," he whispered. "Like you're part of me."

"It's The Inferno. There's a volcano inside me, building toward an explosion." She searched his expression. "Don't you feel it?"

"I feel you. I feel my reaction to you. A need that's clawing me apart. It's like—"

"I have to have you."

"Right now." The words escaped, muffled against her, in a whispered confession. "Resistance is futile?" he quipped.

"Totally futile." She slid her legs upward and wrapped them around his waist. Lifting her hips against his, she groaned. "And totally unnecessary."

Slowly, he rocked to a familiar rhythm, waiting until she caught the beat, then moved faster. Then faster, still. What had started slow and gentle, just a low, relentless burn, became fast and hard and desperate, sending sizzling flames shooting higher and higher. They reached the peak only seconds apart, the moment unlike any she'd ever experienced before. They hovered there in that incendiary moment, unable to move or breathe or speak. Just hang, gripped by ecstasy.

Then they tumbled, falling one against the other, landing in soft satisfaction. And there they drifted until sleep claimed them, wrapped tight together, his hold protective and loving, hers a loving surrender.

"Come on, sleepy head. Time to hit the road." Ty gave Lucia's bare backside a gentle smack that turned into a tender caress.

She groaned. "Too early."

"I know it's early, but we need to move. I'd rather get out of here before the police arrive." He didn't bother to mention the gunmen. No point in starting the day in a panic. "I have breakfast ready for you. You have ten minutes to eat."

Lucia sat up and blinked sleepily. The sheet dropped to her waist and it took all his self-control not to leap back in bed with her and greet the day with an instant replay of the previous night. She definitely made it challenging. He'd never seen anyone more beautiful.

She sat in a swirling sea of fine, brown cotton sheets, her hair tumbling over her shoulders to pool around her hips. Her eyes, intensely blue in that moment, blinked sleepily, sunlight from the windows cutting across them and turning them luminous. Her lips were full and pouty from his kisses, a perfect match for her breasts, which were also full and pouty from his kisses.

She shoved a tangle of curls back from her face. "What's the latest on Nonna?"

He shook his head, hating to give her the bad news. "No change. Still critical. On the plus side, she made it through the night. That's got to count for something."

She nodded, biting her lip for a moment before asking, "Did Juice drop off the car already?"

"And clothes. I left jeans, a shirt, and underwear for you to change into on top of the dresser."

She took that in stride. "Oh, thanks." Her head tilted to one side. "Any chance I have time for another shower?"

She didn't pout or beg or act coy like some women. Just asked a simple question. He'd even bet if he refused, she'd take that in stride, too, which made him only too happy to grant her request. "A quick one."

She took him at his word, scrambling from the bed and making a beeline for the bathroom, giving him a glorious view of a long, tumble of curls caressing the tops of her swaying hips, not to mention, a pert, rounded bottom. Nope, he decided. No time for that.

With a groan of regret, he yanked a travel case from his closet and made short work of filling it with everything he'd need for the next few days. At the last minute, he opened his top dresser drawer and removed the ring that had belonged to his mother, which he kept on a simple gold chain. Even though it brought unspeakable pain, it was all he had left of her. Blanking his memories of their final days together, he slipped the chain over his head and tucked it beneath his shirt.

Fifteen minutes later, they were ready to go. Ty locked up and set the alarm, and the two hastened to a waiting four-wheel drive Jeep Wrangler. Juice had chosen the high-end package that could climb Mt. Everest while cooking breakfast and surfing the internet. Impressive. Seriously impressive.

The Saturday traffic didn't delay them much and they managed to get out of the city with reasonable ease. The Wrangler's GPS gave them the quickest route to the Dantes' compound. About halfway through the drive, Lucia nodded off.

He woke her an hour and a half later by gently rubbing her shoulders. "We're here."

She sat up in one abrupt motion, inhaling sharply, taking a second to orient herself. Once she had, she looked around, blinking. "Oh, wow."

His thoughts, exactly. He drove down the gravel drive to a parking area between a large storage building and equally large workshop.

The two structures stood adjacent to a huge sprawling rough-hewn log building that boasted a pair of stone chimneys. They'd built it right on the lake's edge, two wings angling off from the main section and cantilevering over the water.

Further along the curve of the lake stood a pier and boathouse. In the opposite direction, he noticed a wide sweep of white sand beach that had to have been trucked in since it wasn't native to the area. Tucked into the nearby woods, he spotted individual cabins, though he supposed "cabin" was a bit of a misnomer for the small, elegant houses. No doubt couples who preferred more privacy used those instead of the main residence. He parked with his tail to the buildings, nose toward the road, so they could depart quickly, if necessary.

Exiting the vehicle, Ty popped the trunk and snagged their two bags. "Juice said to go in the main house. We can have any room we want." He spared her a brief glance. "Or rooms."

"Room," she stated unequivocally.

"Fine. Room."

An unsettling need swept through him, the intensity of his desire catching him off guard. He'd never felt this way about a woman before. Never had the connection burrow so deep. Never experienced the overwhelming insistence he keep her close, keep her safe, protect her.

She's the one.

Ignoring the persistent voice, Ty took the lead, entering the silent lake house. "Stay here while I check the place out."

"Forget that. I'm coming with you."

He didn't argue. Instead, he put her behind him as he made a sweep of room after room. The two wings, combined, featured at least a half dozen bedrooms and even more bathrooms, while the main section boasted a massive great room, with thirty-foot ceilings and a huge fireplace. Floor-to-ceiling windows overlooked the lake. Adjacent to the great room they discovered a gourmet kitchen with a sunroom for casual dining that also faced the lake. A more formal dining area had views of the woods, as did the den and game room. Above the kitchen, he even found a private theater.

"Remind me to find my own diamond mine," Ty muttered.

"You and me, both. This place is huge. We don't need all of this for just the two of us. I wonder why they didn't just offer us one of the cabins in the woods."

"*If*... and it's a big unlikely if, the men who attacked the gala found us here, there are plenty of rooms where we can remain barricaded until help arrives."

"It has safe rooms?"

He shrugged. "Not exactly. Just rooms next to impossible to penetrate without some serious firepower."

She shifted closer to him, the unconscious move making him smile. "No offense, but it looked like the gunmen who attacked the gala had serious firepower."

He leaned in, flicking a strand of hair behind her ear. It clung to him for a brief moment and refused to let go, anchoring them together. "They'd need seriouser firepower."

She grinned. "You're familiar with that sort of seriouser firepower?"

"From my military days, yes," he admitted reluctantly.

"Got it. Is that how you know Juice?"

"We bumped up against each other a time or two."

She blew out a sigh. "Juice doesn't talk about his military days. I gather you don't, either?"

"I'd rather not."

"Okay." Her instant acceptance came as a huge relief. She glanced around the theater room. "So, what do we do now?"

He gave it some thought. "Let's choose a bedroom, preferably one that has more than one egress, as well as a safe area. I want to go through the house more carefully with you and determine exit strategies and, if those are blocked, hiding places."

Her face paled and he saw a hint of trepidation darken her eyes. "You're making me nervous."

He pulled her tight, dropping a reassuring kiss on top of her head. "I'm sorry. I wish we could simply relax and enjoy our time here. But we have to put safety first. Fortunately, the Dantes installed an excellent security system."

She pulled back to gaze up at him, her brow knit in concern. "Do you still have the jewelry I wore last night?"

"No. I passed everything off to Juice when he brought the car."

"Well, that's one problem we don't have to worry about." She gestured toward the stairway leading to the kitchen. "Why don't we get your escape scenarios out of the way?"

It didn't take long. He recommended various places she could hide, as well as designated safe spots that would allow her to barricade herself in. Then they went outside and set up meeting areas in the unlikely event they became separated.

He could see her resistance to his instructions. "Lucia, this is just a precaution. I was very careful to make sure we weren't followed on the drive here. No one other than Sev and Juice know we're using the lake house." He spared a glance toward the sky. "And if I'm not mistaken, we're about to get a snowstorm. Chances are, the roads leading here will be closed. My hope is that the police will have the men who did this in custody within the next few days. Not only will that absolve you of any involvement, but we'll figure out how you know the man who shot your brother and Nonna."

As though to prove his point, the first few snowflakes sputtered free from the laden sky. He was pleased to see his words had the intended affect. The strain eased from her face and she even managed a smile. He took her hand in his and pulled her against him. She snuggled in with a sigh.

"I wish I could identify the man. It would make everything so much easier."

"It would, but try not to stress about it." Unable to help himself, he snatched a swift kiss. "Maybe something will occur to you over the next day or two."

They returned to the main house and he led the way to the kitchen. Opening the refrigerator, he found lunch already prepared. He removed the platter of wrapped sandwiches and carried them to the sunroom. Outside the windows, snow continued to fall, a beautiful sight against the view of the lake and surrounding woods. Lucia joined him, carrying a pitcher of lemonade and two glasses.

He lifted an eyebrow. "Lemonade?"

"I know, I know. But someone made it for us and it seems rude not to drink it. I think it's freshly squeezed."

A brief recollection touched him, of fixing a pitcher of lemonade for his mother because he knew she loved it. He grimaced. "I haven't had lemonade since I was a kid."

"Don't you like it?" She gestured toward his face. "You gave me a look. One of those, oh-crap looks."

He shrugged. "Bad memories."

"I'm sorry. Want to talk about it?"

She asked the question with such gentle concern, he couldn't take offense. And though he'd rather keep the incident buried, he'd been accused all too often of shutting people out. Being a loner definitely had its downside. He didn't want to do that to Lucia. For the first time, he decided to let someone in. To open the door, if only a crack.

He took a deep breath, steeling himself against the flood of memories. Bad memories. "I was thirteen or fourteen. Mom had been diagnosed with breast cancer and chemo was kicking her ass," he confessed. "I thought I'd fix her something that would make her feel better. She loved lemonade and used to make it for me all the time."

"So you fixed her some." She reached for his hand and squeezed it. "Did it make her sick?"

"Yeah. She drank it like a trooper and then spent the night throwing up." He released a sigh. "I never fixed it again. I'm not sure I ever drank it again."

She winced. "I'm so sorry, Ty. Understandable that lemonade would bring back such sad memories. Would you prefer something else?"

He shook his head. "It's fine."

"Did she survive?"

He liked that she asked the question without the awkwardness many displayed. "That bout. It came back a year or so later.

That time she didn't make it. She died when I was sixteen."

To Ty's shock, tears glistened in Lucia's eyes. She was so tenderhearted, her vulnerability right there on the surface for everyone to see. How could she have gone through so much disillusionment at the hands of the Dantes and not grown a thicker shell? She needed that shell. Or maybe she just needed someone to protect her, if only from herself.

"What happened to you after she died?"

He pulled back, unwilling to go there. "I survived."

Lucia's brows drew together. "Not on the streets. Tell me you had family and didn't end up living under a bridge."

He shook his head. "No family. I managed, Lucia. And the day I turned eighteen, I joined the military. They became my family, for a while, anyway." Until they were taken from him. "They made me the man I am today."

She offered a smile, one so sweet and compassionate it threatened to tear him apart. "They did a good job."

To Ty's relief, his cell phone rang, putting an end to the conversation, and he immediately answered. "You're on speaker, Juice. What's the latest."

"How's Nonna?" Lucia interrupted.

"Holding on. That's the best anyone can say." He hesitated. "Lucia, you should prepare yourself, girl. With the amount of blood she lost and the trauma she's suffered, it would be challenging for a young person. Nonna is far from young."

"She's also a fighter," Lucia retorted with a sharp edge. "Don't count her out."

"No one's counting her out. But I don't want you to get your hopes up, either."

"My hopes are up." Her voice cracked and she fell silent just long enough to bring it under control. "And they're going to stay up. She needs all of us to be positive and give her every ounce of optimism and good thoughts we possess."

"You're right, Lucia," Juice said gently. "We should all do exactly that."

"Damn right." She gave an emphatic nod, despite the fact Juice couldn't see it, though her tone said it all.

"Any update on the gunmen?" Ty asked.

"Yeah. Good news on that front. The police staked out Lucia's apartment and it paid off big time. One of the crew used her key to gain access. He's in custody and they're in the process of making a deal with him. He's agreed to identify the others who attacked the gala."

"The gunmen found my purse?" Lucia asked in surprise.

"Yeah, apparently you dropped it by the door to the balcony."

Ty nodded. It made sense she lost it right after witnessing her brother's shooting, as well as seeing Nonna bleeding out. "Have the police uncovered anything else of interest?"

"Not that I've heard, but they really need to talk to Lucia."

"Do they still suspect her?"

Her eyes widened. "Still?" she mouthed at him.

Ty gave a dismissive shrug. "Don't worry," he murmured.

"I don't think so. According to my source—"

"Who shall remain nameless?" Ty inserted smoothly.

"Who shall remain nameless," he confirmed with a chuckle. "The guy they have in custody doesn't know her. He was told to go to her apartment and grab her because she could identify the one who organized the robbery."

"Okay, so that confirms that it's someone Lucia knows and will recognize. Anything else?"

"I'll text you the lead detective's name and number. Give him a call. Let's see if Lucia can't help get this buttoned up."

"Will do."

The call ended and Ty studied Lucia. "What do you think?"

"The police believe I'm involved?" she asked unevenly.

"I'm sure they considered the possibility, just like I did," he informed her, keeping his words calm and matter-of-fact. "But since you're not involved, they'll figure that out soon enough, if they haven't already."

Her breath hitched. "So, you believe me?"

"Of course I believe you," he said without hesitation. He crossed to her side and gathered her close. Stealing her chair, he sat with her tight within his hold. "I wouldn't have made love to you last night if I didn't. I may have caved on mixing business and pleasure, but I'm not a total idiot. I did learn something from last time."

She covered her face with her hands, visibly struggling for control. It took her a long moment before she lowered her hands again and rested her head against his shoulder. "Thank you."

"Can you handle talking to the police?"

"Yes."

"I'll be right here with you. I'm going to call the detective and set it up. Just be straight with them."

"Should I have a lawyer?" she asked uncertainly.

"It's certainly an option, but why don't we find out what they want, first. It might not be necessary. If you feel you need one at any point, either during or after the phone call, I'll contact Sev and have him arrange it."

"Okay. Thanks."

Ty continued to hold her while they finished lunch, any excuse to touch her. It eased something deep inside, allowed the tension he'd experienced ever since they first met, to calm. He didn't understand why he needed the constant contact, nor did he probe too deeply into the cause. He simply surrendered to the desire.

Not that Lucia complained. She reacted in an even more blatant manner, finding endless reasons to stroke his hand or arm. Like him, she seemed to delight in each and every skin-on-skin contact.

As soon as they finished lunch, Ty set up the interview. He sat at the table in the sunroom next to Lucia, holding her hand, resisting the temptation to pull her onto his lap again. Right now, thinking straight superseded his more basic biological needs.

After placing the call, they were put on hold for a few minutes, then a cool, dispassionate male voice came over the phone's speaker. "This is Detective Jacobi. Could you please identify yourself?"

"Ty Masterson, Detective. I was hired by the Dantes for their protection detail the night of the gala. I'm here with Lucia Benedict."

"And where is here?"

Yeah, that wasn't going to happen. Not if he could help it. "Could we return to that question at the end of the interview?" Ty temporized.

"Very well." The detective got right down to business. "Mrs. Benedict, could you please give me your full name and date of birth?"

She cleared her throat and a surge of relief swept through Ty that the detective couldn't see the shredded nerves emblazoned on her face. "Please call me Lucia Moretti. My birthday is July 25th. I'm thirty."

"Benedict is your married name?"

Ty stiffened at the question and Lucia shot him a swift, nervous glance. "It was. I'm divorced." She took a deep breath, as though steeling herself. "I jumped into an ill-advised marriage the day I turned eighteen. It lasted less than a year."

"Why are you still using your married name if you've been divorced for more than a decade?"

She blew out a sigh, stirring in obvious discomfort. "When I applied for a job with the Dantes, I didn't want them to know my name was Moretti because they would have recognized it, so I went back to using my married name."

"Please explain that."

"I assume you know I'm Primo Dante's executive assistant?"

"We've been given that information, yes."

"My mother and Primo Dante's son had an affair. My brother and I are the result."

A brief pause ensued. At a guess, the detective was connecting the genetic dots. "So, you're the senior Mr. Dante's granddaughter?"

"Yes. And though they were aware of my brother's existence, they were unaware of mine and I preferred to keep it that way until I got to know them better."

"How long have you been using the name Benedict?"

"About a year."

"That's the only time since your divorce you've used it?"

"Yes." She tilted her head to one side. "Why?"

He ignored the question. "Do the Dantes know who you are now?"

"I believe Nonna knows."

"The woman they shot?"

Her chin trembled. "Yes."

"Where is your ex-husband now?"

She spared Ty a brief glance. "He's dead. On the day our divorce was finalized, he drank himself into a stupor, climbed behind the wheel of a car, and wrapped it around the nearest pole. Fortunately, he didn't take anyone else along with him."

"Have you had recent contact with his family?"

Lucia shook her head. "I'm sorry. Why are you asking about my ex-husband?"

"Please answer the question."

Ty gave her hand a supportive squeeze and she sighed. "No, I haven't spoken to any of them since I left Andrew. They despise me. They blame me for his death."

"Are you familiar with the name Orrin Benedict?"

It took her a moment to come up with the connection. "I think that's Andrew's brother."

"Have you had any contact with him since your divorce from Andrew Benedict?"

"I already told you," she stated evenly. "I haven't had contact with any of the Benedicts. I never even met Orrin. I believe he was in prison during my marriage to his brother."

"Do you know the charge?"

She stilled, snatching up the last of her lemonade and taking a quick sip. "I . . . I believe it was armed robbery."

The detective, covering the receiver, conducted a whispered conversation with his colleague. He ended it with a sharp, "Tough." Then he continued, directing his comments to them. "I'd like to text you a picture, Ms. Moretti. Tell me if you recognize the man."

A moment later Ty's text app pinged and he accessed the photo. It filled the screen and Lucia gasped. "That's Harry. No, no. Henry."

"Detective Andrew, we've both seen this man before," Ty interrupted. "He's a courier who came to Dantes the day before the gala."

"He's come to Primo's office approximately half a dozen times in the last month or so." She shivered. "I didn't like him. There was something off about him."

"That photo is Orrin Benedict."

Lucia's mouth fell open. *"What?"*

"We believe when you began using the name Benedict, it enabled him to track you down."

"Why would he do that?"

"You indicated the Benedicts blame you for Andrew Benedict's death. It might be that simple." He paused for an instant. "We'd like to know your current whereabouts."

Ty spoke before Lucia could say anything. "I appreciate that, Detective. I'd rather not give you that information at this time. We're happy to cooperate with your investigation, but until you've arrested Orrin Benedict, I think the fewer people who know where we are, the better."

"You are aware I can obtain that information."

"I am. I also think you agree with me."

For the first time, the detective allowed a hint of amusement to slide through his words. "We'll be in touch. Please call if you think of anything further that might assist in our investigation."

"Will do."

Ty ended the call and turned his full regard on Lucia. She stirred in reaction, clearly uncomfortable. "You omitted a few details about yourself."

Her gaze slid away. "You mean about my marriage?"

"I mean about your marriage." He could tell from her expression there was more to her story than a foolish teenage marriage. "He was abusive, wasn't he?"

She toyed with her glass of lemonade, which pretty much answered his question. "Why do you ask?"

"Just a suspicion."

She shot him a defensive look. "What? Do I give off some sort of victim vibe or something?"

"No. But marriages don't usually end that quickly unless there's a serious problem."

"You mean other than being young and stupid?"

"Other than," he confirmed.

She maintained her defenses for a whole sixty seconds before they collapsed. "He moved us across the country from Seattle in order to live closer to his family. I had no one when he started to—" She broke off with a weary shrug.

"I'm sorry."

"Me, too." She released her breath in a sigh. "What he didn't count on was Gabe. When my brother didn't hear from me, despite repeated calls, he flew out to New Jersey and drove to our apartment. He took one look at me and had us both on the next plane home."

"I'm looking forward to getting to know your brother better. He sounds like a special man."

"He is." She spared him a brief look. "When he saw the bruises and the way Andrew had hacked off my hair, I thought Gabe was going to end up in jail for murder. Instead, he cried. I'd never seen my brother cry before or since. Not when our father deserted us. Not when our mother died. But he cried because Andrew cut my hair."

Another piece of the puzzle clicked into place. "Is that why you wear it so long now?"

"Yes." Her chin shot up. "It's sort of a screw you."

Ty grinned. "I couldn't agree more. And for what it's worth, I love your hair. It's . . . you."

"It's a pain. But it's also my personal symbol of freedom." She glanced out the window. "The snow is getting heavier."

"I suspect we're going to be snowed in for a few days, though they're calling for a warm spell on Monday, so enjoy it while it lasts." He waited a moment and then said, "It's not your fault."

Lucia's hands curled into tight balls, an outward expression of inner pain. But at least she didn't pretend to misunderstand his comment. "It *is* my fault. Everything that's happened is all my fault. He attacked the Dantes because of me."

"He attacked the Dantes because he's a violent criminal and that's what he's done in the past and will do in the future if he's not stopped. If all he'd wanted was you, he could have taken you out at any time."

She flinched and he instantly regretted speaking with such brutal frankness. "But he wouldn't have come to San Francisco, if it weren't for me."

He pulled her from her chair and into his arms. She nestled against his warmth as though she belonged. "Listen to me, Lucia.

You didn't create Orrin Benedict, any more than you created your ex-husband. For some reason that has no bearing on you, whether through some sort of genetic anomaly or environmental influence or whatever happens to create people like them, the Benedicts grew up to become evil men. The best you can do is to get out of their way."

"And when they won't let you get out of their way?"

He planted a kiss in the middle of the curls on top of her head. "Then you deal with the aftermath, just like we're doing. We hope the police can catch them and put them away for the rest of their lives."

She clutched at his shirt, her face buried against him. "What if Nonna dies? I don't think I can bear it. The Dantes will blame me for her death. *I'll* blame me for her death."

"I don't know the Dantes well, but they seem like reasonable people to me." He tipped her face to his. "Did you have any idea Orrin Benedict planned this?"

"No, of course not," she instantly denied. "If I'd had any suspicion at all, I'd have told someone."

"Were you involved in the robbery in any way?"

Her mouth trembled and hurt burned in her teal eyes. *"No!* I thought you believed me. I would never do anything to hurt the Dantes. They're my family."

"Exactly. They're family. If they have an ounce of common sense, they'll realize you're not responsible for what's happened."

"And if you're wrong?"

He shrugged. "Then I'm wrong. We'll deal with it if it happens. But there's no point in anticipating trouble."

"I thought your entire job was anticipating trouble," she muttered.

He grinned. "You got me there." He cupped her face and took her mouth in a gentle kiss. "But there's a difference between preparing for a possibility and dwelling on something that might not happen."

"I need to stop thinking."

"That would help," he conceded. "Is there anything I can do to make that happen?"

"Yes." She looked up at him, her heart in her eyes. "Ty, would you please make love to me?"

Chapter Seven

Lucia held her breath, praying Ty wouldn't misunderstand the question. She didn't want him to make love to her to provide a distraction. With all that had happened over the last few days, she needed to feel alive, to acknowledge on some level that her world still held meaning.

For a moment, she thought he'd reject her. Make some excuse about her being too fragile or in a compromised emotional state. Granted, there might be a fragment of truth to both of those points. Still, it didn't change one key factor.

The Inferno burned like a white-hot fire, connecting them in ways she couldn't explain. She needed him. Needed him near. Needed him holding her. Needed him deep inside her, completing the connection between them.

Without a word, he ushered her to the master bedroom. For a moment, she thought he'd tumble her onto the bed. Instead, he shoved open a set of French doors leading onto a private balcony that cantilevered over the lake. She gasped at the chilly wind sweeping off the lake.

"Why did you bring us out here?"

He pointed to a spot behind her and she turned to discover a huge hot tub taking up a full third of the balcony. He flipped back the cover and touched a few buttons. Soft lights flickered to life and bubbles churned.

"Strip," he ordered.

She stared in disbelief, turning her face skyward. Snow dotted her skin, the icy flakes melting as fast as they hit. "But, it's snowing. It's freezing."

"Trust me. I'll keep you warm." He proceeded to yank off his clothes, lifting an eyebrow in her direction. In no time, he stood naked in front of her, except for a gold chain he wore around his neck. A small ring, clearly a woman's, hung from it, the sharp glitter of diamonds catching her eye. "Come on, strip. Or would you like me to do it for you?"

She hesitated for another ten seconds, then swiftly undressed. The second the last piece of clothing hit the snow-covered planks of the balcony, Ty helped her up the slippery steps and into the blissful warmth of the hot tub. And then he helped her into the blissful warmth of his embrace.

His mouth closed over hers, his tongue stroking across the seam of her lips. She immediately opened to him, reveling in the power of his kiss. God, she could kiss him all day long and not get enough. He knew just how to move his lips, the perfect amount of pressure, the exact right angle. Aggressive, but not too aggressive. Gentle, but not too gentle. Just sexy as hell.

He cupped her hips, lifting her, then slid her inch by inch onto his erection, stretching and filling her. She groaned, heat surrounding her. Over her. In her. Through her. It made a sharp contrast to the bitter cold swirling across her face and shoulders.

She burrowed against him, the ring hanging from his chain pressing between her breasts. Unable to resist, she kissed a path along the scar he'd received in the train wreck he'd mentioned the first time they'd been together. She hated the thought of his suffering so badly when only a child. Seemed they'd both suffered scars as children, both internal and external.

Then she began to rock, slowly at first, driving them gradually upward. "Ty, you have no idea," she whispered.

"I have every idea."

"I never realized sex could be this good." She laughed and for some reason a hint of tears filtered through the sound. "I can't seem to get enough of you."

"I don't think I'll ever get enough of you, either." He pumped his hips harder and she moved in tempo with the quicker pace. "I don't want to ever get enough."

"I know you don't believe me, but I swear it's The Inferno. It's done something to us. I never wanted a man the way I want you. Never even been tempted."

"Never?"

He didn't mention Andrew's name, and yet she could feel her ex-husband's ghost like a foul breeze between them. A ghost she needed to banish. She cupped his face and gave him a direct look. "I swear to you, I've never experienced anything close to what I'm experiencing with you. Not with him. Not with anyone. What I feel when I'm with you defies comparison. It's like spending a lifetime eating foods without flavor or spice or substance and then tasting the real thing."

"In that case, you've become my favorite flavor."

His arms tightened around her, holding them hip to hip, her breasts sliding across his chest, mouth and lips colliding and clinging. She shuddered, close, so very close. He caught her hands in his, palm to palm. Inferno to

Inferno. The smoldering blaze exploded to life. And then he shifted in just the perfect way, a hard thrust of his hips, sending her careening into oblivion. She went over with a sharp cry and an instant later, he exploded inside of her, filling her.

It took endless minutes to catch her breath. Even longer for her brain to come back online. "I think I've melted," she confessed. "My arms and legs aren't working anymore."

He released her hands and tucked her against him, protecting her from the cold. "They don't need to work. Not yet." He looked down at her and gave her a swift, tender kiss. "Feel better now?"

"Oh, yeah."

"Do you want to talk about him?"

Andrew. So, she hadn't imagined his ghost attempting to come between them. "This once and then he's not worth talking about ever again."

He wrapped her up tight, his hold strong and reassuring. "Tell me and then let it go."

"You already know the end. In retrospect, the beginning is just sad. I mentioned that my father never lived up to his promises. I'd spent years imagining him arriving on our doorstep, marrying my mother, being a real father to me and Gabe. I pretended I was a modern-day Cinderella. He'd gather us up and sweep us away from our miserable little apartment. We'd become Dantes and live in a palace."

"Naturally, none of that happened."

"Naturally. That last time, he showed up when I was fifteen and made endless promises. It was every one of my dreams come true. Then he disappeared. Again. We later learned he'd been killed in a sailing accident. But by then, he'd practically destroyed my family. My mother was never the same. And Gabe . . ." She shrugged. "Gabe became hard and cynical."

"What about you?"

She looked back at the girl she'd been, filled with pity. "I, on the other hand, truly believed my father would fulfill all of my dreams. I lived on that expectation for two whole years. And then, just as I was on the verge of admitting I'd never have a fairy tale life, Andrew showed up."

"How did you meet?"

"I went to a friend's party." She gave an awkward laugh. "A drinking party. If my mom or Gabe had known, they'd have killed me, especially since I was only seventeen and a senior in high school. Andrew was there."

"I assume he was older?"

"Much. He swept me off my feet. I thought I'd finally found my knight in shining armor. Instead, I'd walked right up to a predator and asked him to use and abuse me."

Ty swore, the word vicious. "I wish I'd been there to protect you from him."

"Yeah, well, not even Gabe could protect me. Today, I'd instantly recognize him for what he was. Back then?" She shook her head, filled with empathy and sorrow for the girl she'd been. "I was an idiot."

"You were young and looking for the father you never had." The comment didn't contain an ounce of censure or blame.

"Yeah." She lifted her face to the snowy sky, welcoming the cold wetness that cascaded down on her. "He played all the right angles. Keeping our relationship a secret from my mother and Gabe. Playing the part of Prince Charming. Basically, grooming me, though I was hardly a child."

He pulled her tight against his chest and simply held her. "At seventeen, you were still a child."

"And then I made a fatal mistake. I told him about a fabulous Dante necklace that my father had given my mother on his last visit. It had been one she'd designed for the company years before when she and Dominic first met.

It even had a name, Heart's Desire. It was worth a fortune. The day I turned eighteen, he convinced me to marry him. The next day we left for New Jersey."

"And it went downhill from there." It wasn't a question.

"Yes. I'm not sure why he insisted we get married, other than he figured he'd have a better opportunity to get his hands on the necklace."

"He'd also have more rights over you if you married. That way you'd be tied to him in ways that would be harder to break. And if you inherited the necklace during your marriage, he'd be in the perfect position to claim a portion of it."

It made sense. She forced herself to finish the story as quickly as possible. "The beatings started not long after that. I had no money. No cell phone. Andrew rarely worked. I'm not quite sure where his money came from. Nothing legal, that's for sure. He'd talk about the necklace periodically, tell me to ask my mother to sell it so we could live like royalty. When I refused—" She broke off abruptly. "Let's just say, it got bad."

Ty hugged her tight. "You're safe now. Andrew is dead and can never hurt you again. And soon his brother will be found and dumped back in prison where he belongs."

She curled against him, kissing the dampness from his broad shoulders. "Do you think Andrew told Orrin about the necklace? Maybe that's why he came after me."

"It's possible."

"He can't know we sold it to pay medical bills when Mom became sick."

He stilled. "Cancer?"

She shook her head, wrapping her arms around him. "No, no. It was a really virulent strain of pneumonia. I think after Dominic died, she just gave up and didn't want to fight anymore."

"How old were you?"

"Twenty." She tipped her head back. "I survived just fine. Unlike you, I had Gabe."

"I look forward to getting to know him better."

He'd said that before and the words gave her a surge of hope. If this were just a casual fling or if he still felt the way he had when he'd ended things between them after their first night together, he wouldn't have said that. "It's getting late."

"And you're starting to shiver." He stood, dragging her to her feet. "Go on inside and hop in the shower. I'll grab our clothes and join you in a minute."

Unlike their last shower together, they didn't linger. A quick wash and then they bundled up into warm clothing. "This seems like the perfect evening for a fire." She grinned up at him from beneath the towel covering her hair and half her face. "I don't suppose you know how to start one?"

"As a matter of fact . . ."

"Score! I'll trade you a hot, roaring fire for a hot, somewhat roaring dinner."

"You're on." He glanced down at his hand with a frown, rubbing at his palm. The instant she noticed, he balled his hands into fists.

She folded her arms across her chest. "What's wrong with your hand, Ty?"

"Nothing."

Lucia didn't believe him for a nanosecond. "Bull. You wouldn't have rubbed it unless something was bothering you." She held out her hand. "Show me. Is it The Inferno? Is it burning? Itching?"

He swore beneath is breath. "Not that again. I thought we'd been through this already. There's no such thing as an Inferno."

"Try telling the Dantes. Now show me your hand." He released a long drawn out sigh, the sound so typically "exasperated male" that she almost laughed. He held out his left hand. "Nice try, Masterson. The other hand, please."

"It's just a bruise or a stain or something." He showed her the palm of his right hand. Sure enough, a reddish-purple mark discolored the very center. "It's nothing."

"It's actually rather elegant." She looked closer. "Sort of a curly swirl. It looks a bit like a stylistic half-moon."

"Great. Just what I need. An elegant, swirly half-moon on my palm. Juice will never let me live it down."

She took his hand in hers, gently running her thumb across the mark. "Does it hurt? Itch? Burn?"

"No. No. No."

She eyed him sharply. "Yeah, but there's something. What?"

He hesitated, then confessed, "It tingles when you touch it."

Her brows drew together. "Just when I touch it, or when you touch it, too?"

He drew his hand back and jabbed at the mark. "Huh. Just when you touch it." He cocked his head to one side. "Do it again."

She touched it with her index finger. "Shit," he muttered. "That's bizarre. And before you say it, it's not The Inferno."

"How do you know?"

He scowled. "Do the Dantes have marks on their palms?"

She shrugged. "I don't think so. But then you didn't feel that weird spark when we first touched. Maybe you got this, instead."

"You know I'm crazy about you, right?"

"Really?" She beamed at him. "I'm crazy about you, too."

"Crazy about me, or just crazy?"

Her smile turned to a grimace. "Hey, play nice. I have it on excellent authority that none of my Dante siblings or Dante cousins believed in The Inferno until it happened to them. If you ask them now, they'd all tell you it's real. Every last one. Until I met you, I was the only one who hadn't experienced it."

"You do realize I'm still not buying any of this." He hesitated, his tone softening. "I'm just afraid you're looking for another fairy tale. Another Prince Charming. And I'm definitely not him."

She stepped back as though slapped. "I gave up on fairy tales the day Andrew first hit me," she bit out. "I'm not interested in Prince Charming. I don't want pretend. I want reality."

"And The Inferno is your idea of reality?"

She struggled to find the appropriate words to convince him. Or at least, gain some sort of acceptance. "When we first shook hands, it was as though I'd touched a livewire. Before that happened, if someone asked if The Inferno was real, I'd have said no. The Inferno is just a sweet, romantic myth."

"It *is* just a sweet, romantic myth, honey."

She met his cynical look with an unflinching scowl that had most men backing away. To her amusement he didn't back away. He took a step closer, invading her space. "Listen, my brother Gabe is the most cynical and pragmatic man I know and even he believes in it. Does Sev strike you as someone prone to an overactive imagination? Or someone who believes in fairy tales? Does Luc? They all swear it's real. There are eleven Dante couples who would tell you it exists. We'd be the twelfth. The only one who didn't marry their Inferno mate was my father."

Ty folded his arms across his chest and lifted an eyebrow with a sardonic smile. "And it killed him?"

She released a groan of exasperation. "No, I'm not saying that at all. I am saying he chose to marry for money instead of love and his marriage ended in utter disaster." She mimicked his stance and thrust her chin out for good measure. "Even before I saw you, I sensed you. It was the strangest thing that's ever happened to me."

He stiffened. "What are you talking about?"

She tucked her towel more firmly around her, avoiding his gaze, wishing she'd never mentioned it. If he thought her crazy before, this would confirm it. "I heard a voice," she muttered.

"Come again?"

She lifted her head and glared at him. "I heard a voice, okay?"

To her surprise, he didn't dismiss her comment, let alone ridicule her. "What did the voice say?" he shocked her by asking.

Why would he ask that instead of dismissing the claim out of hand? Embarrassed heat burned a path across her cheekbones. He was really going to make her say the words? Okay, fine. She screwed her eyes closed and spoke fast to get it over with. "It said, *He's here. Take him. Make him yours.* I know it sounds crazy—"

"Sounds crazy?" he interrupted. "Try *is* crazy." He waited a beat, then added, "And what's crazier is that I heard the exact same thing. Maybe the words were a little different, but close enough."

Her eyes popped open and her jaw dropped. "You. Are. *Kidding*. Me."

"I wish I were. Ever since then, I can tell when you're close. It's like I'm sensing you on some level." He turned on his heel in clear dismissal and headed for the bedroom.

Lucia followed right behind. "You can't just leave it there, Ty. I can tell there's more."

He glanced over his shoulder, his features set in grim lines. "It's how I knew you were in the ladies' room right before the gunmen hit the gala. Or more precisely, which ladies' room."

His words impacted like a shot to the solar plexus. "You've felt all that and kept it from me all this time? And you have the nerve to say you still don't believe in The Inferno?"

He yanked on jeans, the ring on his chain swinging wildly. No boxers or shorts. Hmm. Apparently, he'd decided to go commando. Not that she minded. She might try it herself. It would sure make it faster and easier to get naked.

"That sort of stuff doesn't exist," he stated in no uncertain terms.

"Right. So, we're just imagining our connection, the voices, the little GPS feature that allows us to find each other?"

"Yup, that's what I'm saying."

"Got it." She rubbed at her palm, the itch more intense than ever before. She glanced at it with an irritated frown. Then her eyes widened. "Well, I have a pretty fancy mark here that says it does exist."

His head jerked around. "What?"

She held up her hand, palm outward. "Seems you're not the only one with a cute little half-moon tattoo in the center of your palm. I've got its mate."

He reached her in two swift strides, snatching up her hand and staring at the mark. He compared it to his own. "Son of a bitch. They match."

"What do you say now, Inferno Mate?" If her tone sounded a tad smug, she decided it was a reasonable enough reaction. "Still believe there's no such thing?"

He shook his head. "There has to be a reasonable explanation."

She snapped her fingers. "And I know what it is."

"Don't say it."

"It's The Half-Moon, first cousin to The Inferno."

He winced. "Okay, can we table this for the time being?"

"Sure," she said brightly. Wise woman that she was, she sensed she'd scored enough points to let it drop. "Why don't I poke around the refrigerator and see if I can't find something to throw together for dinner."

"And I'll get that fire going."

He snatched up a pullover sweater, tugging it over his head on his way out of the room. She couldn't help wondering why he resisted the idea of The Inferno so hard. Maybe it was just his levelheaded, no-nonsense side coming to the fore.

Lucia slowly dressed, grateful that whoever had obtained clothes for her had gone with long-sleeved layers. All the while, she continued to mull over the various possibilities for why Ty continued to resist The Inferno. Clearly, he shared her brother's practical nature.

Gabe never would have believed in The Inferno if he hadn't felt the burn when he'd first touched his wife, Kat. He'd even flown to San Francisco to meet their grandfather for the very first time, in order to obtain answers. Not that those answers had satisfied him. He hadn't believed a word of it when Primo first explained the family legend, dismissing the possibility out of hand. Not that it changed anything.

The Inferno defied disbelief.

She gathered up their towels, along with the clothes they'd been wearing before their visit to the hot tub and dumped them in the washer. Next, she headed for the kitchen. She found Ty there, opening a bottle of wine and setting it aside to breathe.

"I found steaks in the refrigerator," he informed her.

"Oh, great. The stove has a grill. I'll cook them on that. Are there fresh vegetables I can shish kabob?"

"Red peppers, zucchini, mushrooms, and onions."

Lucia laughed. "My mouth is watering. I don't know about you, but I've worked up an appetite."

His dark gaze heated, burning with an unquenchable hunger. "Make sure you eat well. I'm looking forward to making love to you in front of that fire I have going in the living room."

Warmth filled her belly, shooting through her veins with urgent need. How was it possible when they'd just had sex less than an hour ago? Everything about him drew her. Had her aching with desire. She forced herself to turn away and work on dinner, but her appetite had nothing to do with food and everything to do with him.

The meal didn't take long to prepare. They ate in the kitchen on the stools surrounding one side of a long granite island, chatting about general interests and silly personality quirks. Which side of the bed they preferred. Favorite colors and cars, movies and TV programs. The get-to-know-you bits of detritus that most learned on a first date, but that they'd skipped right over because they couldn't keep their hands off each other.

"Seriously, Scarlett Johansson is your hall pass?"

"Yes, seriously," he replied. "So, who tops your cheat list?"

She gestured with her shish kabob skewer. "No question. Patrick Swayze. I think I've watched *Ghost* and *Dirty Dancing* a hundred times each."

"Swayze? Really?" His brow crinkled. "Not, I don't know, Ryan Gosling or Bradley Cooper?"

"Nope."

"But, wait. Isn't Swayze dead?"

"Yup."

"I'm not sure it counts if he's dead." To her amusement, Ty gave it serious consideration. "Not only that, but if he were still alive, I think he'd be in his sixties."

She slanted him a laughing glance. "Then I guess you don't have to worry about me ending up in bed with him, do you?" She crunched on a lightly grilled sweet pepper still gracing her almost-clean plate. "You on the other hand . . ."

"What if I promised to keep my eyes closed and think of you?"

She shoved her plate to one side. "Yeah, that's just creepy. Plus, Scarlett would probably kick your ass if she found out you were thinking about another woman. I have a feeling she could do it, too. I think she performs most of her own stunts."

He simply smiled. "She can try, though I'm pretty confident I can take a comic book heroine."

Considering his size and wealth of muscles, she probably shouldn't bet against him, Lucia conceded. "I guess if you ever get the chance to use your hall pass, you might as well do it right."

"You mean keep my eyes open and not think about you? So, that's official permission, right?"

She laughed, shoving him off his stool. "Get out of here, Ty."

"Okay, okay. There's only one problem with my choice."

"And what's that?"

"Grab our wine." The minute she did, he swept her off her perch and into his arms. "The problem is, I don't want anyone except you."

She wrapped her arms around his neck and kissed the base of his throat. The glasses clinked and their wine threatened to slosh over the rims. "Ditto."

He instantly caught the reference to *Ghost* and chuckled. "Not even Grandpa Patrick?"

"Not even."

He lowered her to a thick, woolen area rug in front of the fire. He hadn't built it into a roaring conflagration, settling for somewhere between brisk and banked. It sparked and crackled, the trapped moisture causing it to pop periodically. They curled up together, sipping their wine.

"Would you really think of me when you were in bed with Scarlett?"

He snorted. "You're killing me, Lucia. I think that's called a no-win question."

She spared him a sideways look, full of mischief. "Would you like a win-win question?"

He took her glass and moved it to a nearby table, setting his beside hers. "It's always a win-win when I'm with you."

"That's so sweet. Corny, but sweet."

He whipped his sweater over his head and settled down on top of her, resting on his elbows so he didn't crush her. She parted her legs and hooked them over the back of his. The ring on his chain swung toward her and she caught it in her hand.

"What's this?"

If he hadn't been draped across her, she might not have picked up on his tension. At her question, his muscles clenched, even though his expression never changed. "It's a ring."

"Got it. Whose ring?"

He answered readily enough, so apparently that wasn't the source of his tension. "I'm not sure. My mother always wore it on this chain, so I assume my father gave it to her. She insisted I take it right before she died."

Something sounded off. "But . . . ?"

"She said the ring belonged to my father."

She took a moment to analyze the odd wording. "She phrased it just like that? It belonged to your father? Not, your father gave it to me?"

"It belonged to my father."

"Huh." His jaw tightened and he avoided her eyes, a dead giveaway. "There's more, isn't there?"

He rolled off her and onto his back, staring at the ceiling. "Do we have to?"

She sat up, instantly concerned. "Of course not, Ty. You don't have to tell me anything you don't want to."

He released his breath in a slow sigh. "That doesn't seem fair considering how open you've been about your ex."

"Doesn't matter," she insisted. "Seriously, you don't owe me an explanation. We're allowed to choose what to share. We're also allowed to not share."

He nodded. "I'll tell you about it. Might as well get it out into the open."

"Okay." Maybe, okay.

"It's not a big deal." He continued to stare at the ceiling, though now the tension visibly rippling through his body and echoed through the rough tones of his voice, belying his words. "It's just something she said before she died. They were her last words to me."

Not a big deal? She suspected just the opposite came closer to the truth. "What did she say?"

His jaw tightened. "She was dying, Lucia. She couldn't have been thinking straight."

Uh-oh. Whatever his mother had said must have been bad to have had such a devastating impact on Ty and force him to make excuses before he'd even told her those final words. She gently stroked his shoulder. "What did she say?"

"She said . . ." He spoke fast, the words tripping over each other. "She said she loved me and that I'd been a wonderful son to her. And then her final words were, 'I wish I really were your mother.'"

Lucia froze. "Do you think she meant it? Is it possible she adopted you?"

"No idea. I've checked my birth certificate and it lists her as my mother. No father, but she is my birth mother. Then I tracked down a couple of people who knew her when she was pregnant with me. It wasn't easy, but I found them. They've all confirmed she gave birth to a son, although she never identified my father to any of them. She didn't have any family they knew of, so that went nowhere."

"Could she have meant she wished she'd been a better mother?"

He shook his head. "I have no idea."

She glanced down at the chain he wore. "What about the ring? Could you trace that?"

"I don't know. Maybe?"

She curled up beside him, her arms wrapped around him. "I'll tell you what. I'll ask Primo take a look at the ring? He may have some ideas about how to trace it."

"Do you think he would?"

"Definitely." She stroked a hand across his broad shoulders. He was so gorgeous, strong and powerful and unbelievably sexy. And he carried such a heavy weight. "I'm sorry, Ty. Leave it to me to not just break the mood, but totally destroy it."

"You haven't destroyed it." He turned to face her, a sudden urgency sweeping across his expression. "Kiss me and I guarantee we'll get the mood back again."

She didn't hesitate. Cupping his face, she leaned in and slid her mouth across his. He jackknifed upward, flipping her onto her back. With a single kiss, he swept away all thoughts and worries about the past and future, leaving only the two of them caught within this brief bubble of time and space.

He didn't rush, removing her clothing piece by piece. He cupped her breasts, worshiping them with mouth and teeth and tongue. She shuddered beneath each caress, passion an uncontrollable force, driving her like a helpless leaf before a fierce wind.

Their lovemaking changed, shifted to something she'd never experienced before. Of course, everything about their relationship was unlike anything she'd ever experienced before. Emotions flooded through her, the incandescent heat of desire, that was a given. But he also infused his taking with a tenderness that stole her breath . . . and her heart.

She'd never believed in love at first sight. Not even Andrew had taken her over and under so quickly. But with one touch, Ty captured her. Held her in the palm of his hand where The Inferno burned fiercest. Made her heart his.

They made love on and off throughout the night until the early morning light bathed them in warmth, and sleep finally claimed them.

Just before Lucia surrendered to oblivion, she pressed her mouth to his and conceded the undeniable truth, if only to herself.

She'd fallen in love with Ty.

Chapter Eight

Ty made certain the next day passed in a haze of pleasure, with no time for fear or worry to intrude. He filled the hours with endless activities, from building a snowman to watching movies and eating popcorn in the Dantes' theater to "playing" in the hot tub. When evening settled, they worked together preparing dinner, talking and laughing about anything and everything—except those few subjects they both deemed off limits.

Even so, time slipped past, and he sensed events moving in a direction that would soon force their return to reality. That night, they made love with a bittersweet desperation, awareness seeping in that morning would bring a sea change neither wanted.

Sure enough, early the next day the insistent ring tone of Ty's cell phone assaulted them, as penetrating as the screech of a fire alarm.

"What the f—?" He bolted out of bed and pawed through the pile of clothes they'd tossed to one side. "What? Who? What time is it? *Shit.*"

"Wakey-wakey, Masterson. It's Juice. It's eight o'clock Monday morning. And right back at you, son."

Ty groaned, struggling to blink the blur from his eyes. Beside him, Lucia stirred and groaned. "No," she pleaded. "Not yet. I need more sleep. Don't you people ever sleep?"

"You conscious?" Juice asked with surprising patience. "Faculties pinging to life?"

"One or two," Ty growled.

"Well, get them all up and running. You're ordered back to San Francisco pronto."

"Why?" he demanded. "What's happened?"

"Ah, now there's the Masterson we all know and love. Nonna is asking for Lucia."

His brain finally came online, the world around him becoming sharp and clear. "She's improved?"

"Would love to say yes." A grim quality underscored the comment. "I truly would."

Ty reluctantly shook his head at Lucia's hopeful expression. He sat on the edge of the bed and slung an arm around her shoulders. He wished they weren't both naked during this conversation. Even though they couldn't be seen, it felt awkward. Still, he'd been in far more awkward situations, some of them involving Juice.

"Seriously, what's going on?"

"Primo wants her back, like yesterday. And when Primo speaks . . ."

"Everyone obeys."

"You got it."

Ty stood and walked to the bank of windows overlooking the lake. Despite the forecast for a warm snap, snow still blanketed the landscape. "FYI, we're snowed in."

"Hell, son, I rented you a four-wheel drive Wrangler with every bell and whistle known to mankind. I'm confident you know how to drive one of those through a little dusting of snow."

Ty gave serious consideration to the twelve inch dusting. "Of course."

"Then stop wasting my time and get the little miss to the hospital."

He spared the "little miss" a quick glance. "I'm assuming you know the police have identified Orrin Benedict, Lucia's ex-brother-in-law, as the gunman?"

Juice cleared his throat. "I might even have known before they did."

Of course he had. "Are they any closer to finding him?"

"Not, yet."

Ty took a deep breath and thought through what he needed to do and how best to accomplish it. "I'll call you when we're twenty minutes out. Meet us at the hospital. I want Lucia escorted inside. No point in taking any risks."

"That's the game plan. And just so you know, that game plan includes your joining Lucia when she visits Nonna."

"Primo's orders?"

"Are there any other kind?"

"We'll be there as quick as we can," he confirmed, checking the time. "We're looking at closer to four or five hours than three."

"The clock is ticking." Juice's voice turned grim again. "We don't know how much longer she's going to last."

"We'll be on the road within thirty."

"I'll let everyone know."

One final question occurred. "Juice, do you know why she wants to see Lucia?"

"Yes."

With that, the call disconnected, leaving Ty swearing beneath his breath. After Lucia's initial question about Nonna, she'd remained silent throughout the conversation. He appreciated her restraint.

"It was Juice, obviously. Nonna is asking for you and they'd like us to get to the hospital as soon as possible." He hesitated. Should he tell her they didn't expect her grandmother to last much longer? As much as he hated doing it, it wouldn't be fair to conceal the information. "They don't know how much time she has," he added gently.

Lucia nodded, taking the news stoically, though he caught the glimmer of tears. "Do you know why she wants to see me?"

"No idea. You?"

"Possibly." She jumped to her feet. "We have clothes in the dryer, and I'd like to grab a two-minute shower."

"I'll fix breakfast. I want to be on the road in thirty."

"No problem."

He watched her scurry, naked, in the direction of the laundry room. No problem, she'd said. He didn't know a single woman who could pull herself together, shower, pack, eat, and hit the road in under thirty minutes.

Except Lucia, apparently.

They actually managed it in twenty. Leaving the Dantes' compound took the longest, the road slippery and difficult to negotiate. The county roads leading to the highway were in slightly better shape due to a continuous stream of slow-moving traffic. US 5 was wet, but hadn't received any snow at all. He made up for lost time there, willing to eat a ticket if it meant getting to San Francisco a little sooner.

He called Juice, as planned. Pulling up to the entrance, he waited until Dante security identified themselves and shepherded Lucia inside. After parking the Wrangler, he joined the small group, impressed despite himself. He doubted the president commanded a better detail than the one assigned to Lucia.

They were dropped off at a waiting area outside the ICU. After a few minutes, Sev exited the unit and joined them, holding out a hand to Ty. "Thanks for everything you've done for us, Masterson. Both watching over Lucia and getting her here in time to see Nonna."

In time. He glanced toward Lucia and saw her visibly flinch at the words, her face turning bone white. He took her hand in his and she clung to him as though he'd thrown her a lifeline.

"Should we go in now?" she asked in a strained voice.

Sev hesitated, his gaze sharp and assessing. He knew, Ty realized. He'd been told Lucia was his sister. "Primo is in there and normally, they only allow two visitors in the ICU at a time. They're making an exception for Nonna." He offered a gentle smile and his hand twitched, as though he wanted to offer some form of physical comfort. "We don't want to take advantage of the situation, so you won't be able to stay for longer than a few minutes."

Lucia gave a stilted nod. "Okay." She finally looked directly at Sev, openly steeling herself. "Do you know what she wants?"

A slow, amused smile cut across the seriousness of his expression before fading. "Yes." He spared a brief glance in Ty's direction. "I'll let Nonna and Primo explain."

Ty swore.

"Unless you want a smack to the back of the head, I wouldn't let Primo hear you say that." Sev's smile faded, replaced with compassion. "Good luck, sis."

She caught her lip between her teeth. Then without a word she rushed across the room and gave Sev a long, hard hug. "There's no time to talk now," she whispered. "Just know that I'm sorry I didn't tell you sooner."

He rubbed her back. "It's okay. We know now, and we'll definitely make time for a sit down later. Hang in there, Lucia."

The door opened again and Primo stood there. He appeared to have aged half a century since Ty last saw him. A stark white bandage covered one side of his forehead and he clutched a cane, leaning heavily on it. *"Vieni con me, per favore,"* he murmured, as though too exhausted to even attempt his request in English.

"He wants us to go with him," Ty interpreted.

Without a word, Lucia crossed to her grandfather and took his hand in hers. In a simple, infinitely loving gesture, she lifted his gnarled fingers to her lips and tenderly kissed them. Tears streaked down his weathered face and he gathered her close. *"Mia cara nipote."*

No question, the cat was definitely out of the bag. Ty wondered who had revealed her true identity? Gabe? Nonna, herself? Or possibly the police. Not that it mattered. The fact that the Dantes accepted her so openly and with such generosity filled him with relief.

Primo escorted them down a short corridor and through a sliding door into a small cubicle. Nonna lay there, hooked to endless machines, all blipping and beeping. No breathing tube, he noted, an encouraging sign. Lucia instantly crossed to sit on the edge of the bed and took her grandmother's hand in hers.

Ty gazed at the woman lying there. She appeared so tiny and helpless. A halo of soft, white curls surrounded her head, most of them confined to a long braid someone had threaded with a decorative ribbon. Her face was as white as Lucia's, throwing into prominence her delicate bone structure. And that's when it struck him.

"Lucia looks just as my sweet Julietta did when I first set eyes on her," Primo said in a gruff whisper, apparently reading Ty's mind. "Her hair was long, as well, tumbling past her hips in curls that were every shade of brown known to man. She was a tiny Venus. Perfection given life."

"You know who Lucia is."

Primo chuckled, a mere shadow of his usual laugh. "Always. From the moment my *nipote* walked into my office for the interview, I knew who she must be. It was my bride, young once more. If not for the eyes, I would have sworn she was my Nonna. And the look in my poor granddaughter's gaze. Such a tragic combination of hope and suspicion, anger and longing. So, I played her game and waited. I think she was close, yes?" His face crumbled. "Close to confessing her true identity."

"Very close." He had no idea if it were true. The need to console outweighed the harm of such a small lie. "We were told Nonna has a request."

"Hear me, boy." Primo suddenly turned on him, his unexpected aggression catching Ty off guard. The old man switched to Italian, a lion defending his pride, his voice so soft Ty could barely make out the words. But the sheer ferocity came through as though he shouted. "You will honor this request my Nonna makes. You will do as she asks, do you understand me?"

"What is her request?"

Primo hacked a hand through the air. "No! There is to be no discussion. No hesitation. She will ask, you will agree. After . . ." He swallowed, his words faltering for the first time. "After we will negotiate, if we must. *Capisci?*"

"*Capisco.*"

Primo approached the bed, making heavy use of his cane. He gently stroked Nonna's hair. "*Amore mio,* Lucia is here, my precious one."

Nonna's lashes fluttered, and her gaze drifted toward Primo. A wealth of love filled her hazel eyes. She murmured something too soft to hear, but whatever she said had Primo wiping a tear from his cheek. Ty felt like an intruder, even more so when Nonna turned and squeezed Lucia's hand.

"You came," she said simply.

Lucia leaned in, brushing her lips across the pale, paper-thin curve of Nonna's cheek. "Of course I came. I will always come whenever you call me."

The older woman struggled to catch her breath, gathering her fading energy. "I made a request of you at the gala." Lucia's eyes widened in alarm and Ty froze, fighting the instinct to cross to her side and protect her. Protect her from what? A dying woman lying in a hospital bed? "Do not pretend with me, child. You remember the request."

"Yes, I remember."

Nonna glanced toward Ty. "I wish to see the two of you wed before my life ends."

"Married?" At Ty's unthinking question, Primo shifted, the lion stirring.

"Here in this room." Her hand swept across the thin sheet and blanket covering her, her fingers plucking at the folds. "As soon as it can be arranged."

"They will marry in just a few short hours," Primo spoke before anyone else could. He shot Ty a hard look. "Your appointment to pick up your license to marry, it is in an hour."

Regardless of his preferences, Ty couldn't argue, just couldn't. The fact that he'd been backed into a corner didn't matter. Whether or not he wanted to marry or preferred to remain a lone wolf didn't matter. The speed and recklessness of the marriage didn't even matter. The bottom line was, he couldn't bring himself to break the heart of a dying woman.

"We won't be late," he stated with false calm.

"You will return here as soon as you have the license. Our priest will be waiting to conduct the service."

Ty lifted an eyebrow. "He's agreed to do it at the hospital?"

Primo shrugged. "He has known the family for a very long time. He will make an exception for us."

"That's some pull."

"Yes. I have some pull." He glanced down at Nonna and frowned. Her eyes had fluttered closed and her breathing grew fast and shallow. "She needs her rest. We will see you in a few hours."

"We'll be back as quickly as possible," Ty promised.

Juice arranged for them to have an escort on their drive to the courthouse, just as a precaution. Ty couldn't decide whether to be amused or concerned. Since he wasn't allowed to bring his weapon into the government building, he stowed it in the glove compartment. With Juice parked directly behind him, it should be safe enough.

He glanced at Lucia. "Are you ready to do this?"

"I was going to ask you the same question." She moistened her lips. "Ty—"

"Yes, we do."

She blinked. "We do?"

His hands tightened on the steering wheel of the Jeep. "Yes, we do need to go through with the marriage."

"Okay." She shot him an apprehensive glance. "Why?"

"You know why." He shot her a fierce look. "For God's sake, Lucia, it's her dying wish. You think I'm going to refuse your grandmother's dying wish? No way. I won't have that hanging over my head."

She sighed. "I would understand if you did refuse. After all, she's not your grandmother. You don't owe the Dantes anything."

Fury shot through him and he struggled to tamp it down. "You'd understand my being a total bastard? Just great. Should I be flattered?"

She clutched her hands in her lap. "You know I didn't mean it that way," she whispered.

His anger dissipated as quickly as it had flared. This wasn't her fault and he shouldn't take it out on her. "I know, I know." He turned toward her, struggling to understand. "Listen, we have a few minutes before our appointment. Let's talk about this. Nonna said she made a request at the gala. And I overheard her talking about marriage. Care to fill me in?"

"You thought she was talking about Gabe."

His mouth curved up at one corner. "Not Gabe, I assume."

She laughed, though a hint of strain threaded through the sound. "Definitely not Gabe."

"She was talking about me."

"Yes."

His eyes narrowed. "Why? Why would she insist you marry me? It doesn't make any sense. I never met her before that night at the gala. Yet, she shakes my hand and informs you that we have to marry? That's insane."

Nerves tripped over her features, alarm combined with reluctance. She didn't want to answer his question, and he realized they should have discussed this long ago. Maybe they would have, if the time since the gala hadn't sent them spinning from one crisis to the next.

"Answer me, Lucia." The request—*order*—came out sharper than he'd intended, but it had the desired effect.

She snatched a swift breath and confessed, "Nonna realized I'd experienced The Inferno with you and she insisted we marry."

Lucia darted Ty a swift glance, flinching from his reaction. He appeared both outraged and shocked. Worse, he clearly didn't believe a word of it. She dug her thumb into her palm, feeling the familiar itch and burn centered there.

"How?" he demanded. "How did she know?"

She shook her head, helpless to explain it. "I have no idea. I never said anything about The Inferno when we first met. I hadn't even told her about our relationship, what little there was at the time."

"And yet, she knew all of those things." He ticked the points off on his finger. "She knew you were her granddaughter although, based on what Primo told me, it wasn't as big a secret as you thought."

"Say what?" Shocked, she could only stare for a moment. "Primo *knew?* How is that even possible?"

"Apparently, you look just like Nonna did at your age. He said he recognized you the moment you walked into his office."

Lucia took a moment to digest that. "My grandparents are absolutely amazing."

She barely stumbled over the reference, unused to claiming their relationship. Now that she'd said the word aloud, it resonated, sliding deep inside and taking root. Ty continued to tick off his points.

"She knew you'd experienced The Inferno. She even knew I was your supposed Inferno mate. Explain it to me, Lucia."

"I know, I know," she moaned. "It sounds crazy when you list it like that."

"Why was she pushing so hard for marriage? Why is she still pushing?"

Lucia tucked her hair behind her ears, amazed it hadn't knotted into a tangled mess, especially since it hadn't seen so much as a drizzle of conditioner in days. "I think she's pushing because of my parents. When Nonna and I spoke at the gala, she reminded me of their experience with The Inferno, that they didn't marry when it struck. She didn't want the same thing to happen to us."

"How did she know about us?" he repeated.

"I told you. She has the eye."

He rubbed his face with both hands, for the first time betraying a hint of exhaustion. Not surprising considering all that had happened over the course of the past few days. Especially considering how little sleep they'd gotten the last two nights. To her relief, his anger seemed to have faded, not that the small explosion had frightened her.

The realization caught her off guard. She'd never once questioned her safety during her time with him, and she doubted she ever would. He didn't rouse that instinctive flight or fight response that had defined her life with

Andrew. Just the opposite, in fact. If she ever felt afraid, Ty would be the first person she turned to.

"I gotta tell you, your family is a bit nutty," he said after a moment.

"Yeah, I'd like to argue that, but I can't."

"So, Nonna has the eye. And her eye told her you'd experienced The Inferno with me. You realize how crazy all that sounds?"

Lucia flipped up her hand and pointed to the stylistic reddish-purple "half-moon" decorating the center of her palm. "Talk to me about crazy. I dare you."

"Touché." His cell chimed and he glanced at it, blowing out an exasperated sigh. He opened his text app and thumbed a rapid response. "Juice. He wants to know—and I quote—what the effing hell are you two doing? Quit stalling or I'm under orders to escort you inside, personally. Bruises will be involved if I have to get out of this mfing car."

Lucia peered over his shoulder, her eyebrows climbing upward. "If Primo saw that, he'd have a few choice words with Juice over his language."

"I don't think it's Juice who'd be the subject of Primo's wrath," he said drily.

"Good point." She spared him a swift, nervous glance. "So, are we going through with this or not?"

He didn't hesitate. "Yes, we're going through with this."

"So, forward?"

"Forward." He spared a glance in his rearview mirror. "Though, I have a funny feeling Juice would love it if I made him get out of his mfing car. Have you seen the size of his fists?"

"They're impressive." She patted his hand, biting the inside of her cheek to keep from laughing. "Yours are fairly impressive, too. They may not be as big as Juice's, but I'm sure they're plenty big enough."

He slanted her an amused glance at the teasing reassurance. "Even so, I'd rather not be on the wrong side of Juice's meathooks."

"Don't worry, I'll protect you."

He slammed her with a single look. "That is definitely not happening. You're not coming between me and Juice. Ever," he emphasized. "Or anyone else, for that matter. It's my job to keep you safe, not the other way around."

She pretended to shiver. "I just love it when you go all Tarzan on me."

"No problem. If you want some Tarzan action, just wait until tonight."

"Our wedding night." The words escaped without thought, and they both glanced in the direction of the courthouse building.

For some reason, the description didn't rouse the dread he anticipated. Up until now, he'd always considered matrimony a bit of a trap. This time, the thought filled him with a far different emotion. Something to consider further. Not now. Maybe not for another couple years. On second thought, maybe he wouldn't think about it at all. If he'd learned one thing in the military it was not to spend too much time anticipating what couldn't be controlled or changed. The only way through was through.

"Come on. Juice is stirring. Let's disappoint him."

It didn't take them long to find the appropriate office and fill out the papers required by the city clerk. As soon as they paid for the license, Ty steered them out of the building and back to the Wrangler. "We have one more stop before returning to the hospital."

"What's that?"

He took a moment to research where they could find what they needed and texted Juice their next location, as well as a single wedding request. Satisfied, he glanced at Lucia, finally answering her question.

"I don't know about you, but I'd rather not get married in jeans. I found a local place where we can get something better suited to a wedding."

A faint flush touched her cheeks. "Thank you. That's really thoughtful."

"No problem."

"All part of the hero package?"

"You got it." He started the car and put it in gear. "We can negotiate any surcharge later tonight."

Was she blushing? She touched her heated cheeks. Yeah, she was blushing.

The store he'd chosen offered a his and hers section and while the attendant ushered him in one direction, Lucia headed in the other, disappearing behind racks of lace, silk, and tulle. Every once in a while, he'd catch the sound of a laugh or an excited, "oooh!" or eager chatter between her and the saleswomen. Then silence. Prolonged silence.

Ty checked the fit of his suit in the mirror. Satisfied, he crossed the no man's land between the two sides of the boutique and stopped dead in his tracks. Lucia stood on a raised platform in front of a trifold mirror, her back to him. They'd gathered her hair at the nape of her neck in a complicated series of braids and loops he longed to unknot.

She wore a rich cream colored, three-quarters length dress that fit from bodice to hips, then fell to her calves in soft, loose pleats. The back dipped low, baring her gorgeous spine. But the pièce de résistance was the waist-long beaded necklace that encircled her throat and then draped backward, down the curve of her dress to caress her supple back, twitching and flirting with her every move.

She turned to face him and his hands clenched into fists. *Dear God.*

The dress clung and clung and clung, making him long to explore every inch of the path it traversed from fragile collarbone to rounded hips. He didn't think he'd ever seen anyone more stunning. *Mine. Take her. Take the woman.* Oh, hell, yeah, he told the voice. I'm going to take her. He crossed to stand in front of her and held out his hand. She slipped hers into his and shuddered.

"Hearing voices?" he asked with a knowing smile.

"Oh, hell, yeah," she said, parroting his thoughts.

She smiled with such radiance, it knocked every thought from his head except one. To pull her into his arms and never let her go. "Ready to get married, Lucia Moretti?" He deliberately omitted her bastard ex's name.

She took a deep breath. "I'm ready. What about you?"

He waited for any sense of hesitation or opposition. Considering the marriage had been forced on them, it wouldn't be surprising. Instead of resistance, an odd urgency filled him.

"All set," he announced. After arranging for payment, he escorted her to the door. "Let's get back to the hospital."

He helped her into the passenger seat, checking to make sure her dress didn't hang outside the door. Circling the Wrangler, he climbed behind the wheel. He spared a swift glance in his rearview mirror to make sure Juice was still with him. Satisfied, he pulled into traffic and worked his way back to the hospital.

The car that hit them came out of nowhere. Just before their turn into the hospital parking lot, it slammed into the rear driver's door and whirled them around in two full 360s. Even as the car spun, Ty grappled for the glove compartment and his gun. The Wrangler hadn't come to a full stop before he had his gun in hand and a round chambered. Then he dove from the car and vaulted over the hood, to snatch at Lucia's door.

"Release your seatbelt," he shouted. "Hurry! Release it!"

It took her two tries to hit the button to open the clasp. The instant she had, he tossed her out and onto the ground, crouching in front of her. Beads burst around them, scattering. Then movement seemed to stutter, shifting to slow-motion. Even the beads appeared to slow their arching bounce and clatter.

Juice's vehicle slewed to a stop and men piled out on all sides. A sharp ping impacted beside Ty's head, followed by another that hit the passenger door window right where Lucia had been. An instant later, the window exploded, raining down on them, the sting of broken glass cutting his hands and the side of his face. A sea of glass shards and beads surrounded their tiny oasis of safety, and all the while one fact remained uppermost in his mind. If Lucia had still been inside, those two shots would have taken her out, no question.

He opened fire. Out of his peripheral vision he saw Juice drop to one knee, followed by the rapid pop-pop-pop of a Glock, reverberating sharply off the walls of the surrounding buildings.

"Go, go, go!" shouted Juice. "He's down. He's down. Benedict is down."

Ty scooped up Lucia and ran toward the hospital with her. Security came tearing out from the building as they ran in. Sirens sounded in the distance. He ignored it all, his full focus on the woman in his arms. A number of people shouted to him from the reception area. He bypassed them, darting into a hallway out of the line of sight—and fire—of the entryway.

He crouched down, sweeping his hands over Lucia. "Are you hurt?"

She stared at him, clearly in shock, her eyes wide, pupils blown. "Shooting. He was shooting at us."

There were minor smears of blood on her face and back. A few on her dress, along with black streaks from her contact with the road surface. But nothing that indicated a wound of any kind.

"It's okay. Juice got him. He can't hurt you, anymore. Just hang in there a little longer. We'll get you checked over and make sure you're not hurt."

"I'm not." She shivered. "I'm okay."

Her shiver turned into flat-out shaking and a few remaining beads tumbled off the nearly naked string of her necklace and bounced across the floor. He took a swift peek around the corner of the hallway, spotting a strong police presence. They'd be coming in a minute and he'd rather not give anyone cause to believe him an associate of Benedict. He stripped down his Glock and set it several feet away from where they crouched. Then he pulled Lucia into his arms and held her.

"When the police come, put your hands up." She turned glassy eyes on him and he regarded her in concern. "They'll need to see we're unarmed. Once they identify us, everyone will calm down. But a shootout in front of a hospital is going to put everyone on edge. Do you understand, honey?"

"Yes. Put my hands up. Just like on TV."

"Just like that," he confirmed. "They're coming."

He pulled out his ID and concealed weapons permit, and set both on the floor beside him. Raising his hands, he nodded at Lucia, who copied him. The next moment, police swarmed into the hallway. A few tense minutes followed before they sorted everything out. The instant they were satisfied and had confiscated his weapon, he asked for medical staff to examine Lucia.

The officer in charge immediately agreed. "Then we're going to need you both to come with us."

"We're supposed to get married," Lucia said. "We're supposed to get married before Nonna—" She burst into tears.

Ty wrapped her up in a tight embrace. "Her grandmother, Julietta Dante, is in the ICU. The family has arranged for us to marry there so Nonna can witness the nuptials. Time is of the essence."

Every last officer appeared sympathetic, but it didn't change anything. After he and Lucia were checked by the medical staff and their various cuts and scrapes treated, they were escorted to the police precinct and made comfortable in a stark conference room.

The hours ticked by, the increasing stress on Lucia's face keeping time with each passing minute. At long last they were interviewed, then informed that all of the gunmen from the gala were in custody or dead and Ty and Lucia were allowed to leave. The instant they stepped outside, he called Juice. When it went to voicemail, he dug out Sev's number.

"Where are you?" Sev asked without preamble.

"Just leaving the precinct. We're going to catch a cab back to the hospital." He spared Lucia a brief glance. "Nonna?"

"Holding her own. The priest is on his way." Realizing how that might be misinterpreted, he added, "To perform the wedding ceremony."

"Got it." After giving Lucia the thumbs up, Ty waved down a cab and helped her in. "Is Juice okay?"

"Fine. Just finishing up with the police."

"That's a relief. We should be there in thirty."

The instant he closed the cab door, he pulled Lucia into his arms and simply held her. His name escaped her in a pained whisper, and he lifted her face to his and tenderly kissed her. "It's going to work out."

"I don't see how that's possible."

"I know, but we'll figure it out as we go along." He shook his head with a sigh. "I'm sorry your beautiful dress is wrecked."

She plucked at a rip along her hip and touched the dried smatter of blood and streaks of dirt marring the pleated skirt. Then she shoved at her hair. The pretty knot hung halfway down her back. "I'm a mess."

"You're definitely a mess," he confirmed with a tender smile. "So am I. The important thing is that we're both alive. I'm sure you can borrow a comb and maybe wash some of that blood out."

"We're going to shock the priest."

"I guarantee, we won't. I can also guarantee he's witnessed worse." He kissed her again, needing the constant reassurance that she remained safe and unharmed within his hold. "Even after everything you've been through, you're still the most beautiful woman I've ever seen."

Doubt filled Lucia's eyes and Ty realized she needed more reassurance. He could think of only one way to convince her. Without a word, he lifted her face to his and kissed her again, instantly taking her under.

He kissed her as though she were his everything. As though she were the light, his light, in a sea of darkness. His moon and stars and sun. The very air he breathed.

He consumed her. Marked her. Turned their world upside down and right side up again, so there was no beginning. No end. Just the two of them forged into one. She surrendered to him. Or did he surrender to her? In that moment, a single truth crystalized, slicing straight through to his very soul.

No matter what he'd told her earlier, he loved her. Now and always, she was his.

Chapter Nine

Lucia hurried into Nonna's hospital cubicle, Ty's kiss a hot brand on her lips and on her heart. Even on her very soul. As much as she wanted to consider all the implications of that thought, worry scraped like a dull blade over her emotions. The instant she saw her grandmother, her tension dissipated.

Though she remained pale and frail, she didn't appear to have gone any further downhill. Her breathing remained steady, the blip of her heartbeat on the machine by her bed sounding normal and regular. Primo dozed in a lounger beside her bed and Lucia almost melted to see their hands clasped tight. Ty came to stand behind her, a massive, warm bulwark. Her protector.

For the first time a tiny fragment of hope blossomed within. Maybe, just maybe, Nonna would survive. It happened. People who'd been deemed terminal or on the verge of death had made miraculous recoveries. If anyone were capable of that sort of turnaround, Lucia would bet every dollar in her bank account, Nonna was one.

At their advent, Primo blinked, jackknifing upright. "You have returned." His brows drew together at the sight of them. "A bit the worse for wear, yes? Why is this?"

Ty responded for them both. "Let's just say that the men who attacked the gala are no longer a problem."

Primo nodded repeatedly and the muscles in his jaw clenched and unclenched from the effort it took to maintain a stoic facade. "Okay. This is good," he said at long last, his voice far gruffer than usual. "This is very good. Now they will pay for what they did to my Nonna."

A moment later the priest entered, and to Lucia's shocked delight, her brother followed right behind, one arm in a sling. "Gabe!" Fighting tears, she started to hug him, then hesitated.

"Come here." He threw his good arm around her and pulled her tight. She hadn't realized how badly she needed to see and touch him until he walked into the room.

"I can't believe you came," she whispered against his broad chest.

"Thank God you're all right. Juice just finished filling me in about everything." He lifted his gaze to Ty's and instantly stuck out his good hand. "Thank you for protecting my sister. And thank you for letting me know about today. I wouldn't miss it for anything."

Lucia glanced over her shoulder. "You contacted Gabe?"

Ty nodded. "I asked Juice to do it. You'd have regretted it if Gabe hadn't attended our wedding."

Until that moment, it hadn't even occurred to her. And yet, he was absolutely correct. It wouldn't be the same without her brother.

"We've been given special permission for everyone to be here," the priest offered. "But the hospital staff is not happy. They've asked us to make the ceremony as brief as possible."

Primo stood and kissed Nonna's forehead. She woke with a smile, her gaze going straight to his. Her breath escaped in a long sigh. "I am still here, I see."

"You are still here, *tesoro.*"

She peered around the room, taking in all those gathered around her bed. "It is my hope you are all here for a wedding and not a funeral."

Lucia choked, fighting back tears. "A wedding, Nonna. Definitely a wedding."

Nonna smiled gently at her. "Do you think I am afraid to die?" She shook her head, the motion barely visible. "I am not afraid. The only thing that will be difficult to bear is leaving my Primo behind. He has been at my side from the time I was but an eighteen-year-old girl. But even our parting is only temporary. We will be together again. We all will. Of this I am certain."

"But not yet," Primo insisted gently. Then he looked around the room with a hint of alarm. "Rings? Do you have rings?

Ty reached beneath his shirt and removed the chain he wore. Unlinking the ends, he allowed the ring his mother had given him to drop into his palm. It rested there, a protective circle of gold and diamonds surrounding the odd half-moon swirl centered in the middle of his hand.

Primo inhaled sharply. "What is this?" he demanded.

Ty eyed him warily. "The ring?"

"The ring, yes. And this mark you bear?"

"The mark just showed up recently," he reluctantly admitted. "Lucia has one, too."

"Show me." Ty crossed to the old man's side, hand outstretched. Primo took the ring and gave it a swift, startled look. Then he examined the mark, retaining the ring. "And yours, Lucia?"

"They're the same," she offered, holding her hand out, as well. "I guess we touched something we shouldn't have."

"Or something you *should* have," Primo murmured. He patted her hand and turned his attention to the ring, lifting an eyebrow. "And this, Ty Masterson? Tell me how you came to have this ring in your possession?"

"My mother said it belonged to my father."

Primo backed away, dropping into the lounge chair by Nonna's bed, holding out his hand. "Look, *amore mio.* Look at the ring."

She studied it for a moment, then lifted her gaze to Primo's. Lucia would have sworn they conducted a lengthy and detailed conversation with that one look. To Lucia's shock and amusement, he pulled out a loupe and examined the ring with meticulous care. "Really, Primo? You're going to check to see if the diamonds are real? Here? Now?"

"Oh, they are real."

He took a deep breath and pocketed the loupe, then leaned in close to Nonna, whispering a question in her ear. After a long moment, she nodded. "I have seen it. They may marry."

"Very well." He spared Ty a brief, fierce look, his golden eyes flashing like fire, then repeated. "Very well, though you both should know, I do not believe this marriage will take."

Beside her, Ty bristled. "Just what the hell do you mean by that?"

Primo shrugged, his mouth curving into an enigmatic smile. "I meant what I have said. And I will say no more." He waved his hand toward the priest. "Please proceed, Father Benito."

The priest hesitated, frowning. "Do you object to this wedding, Primo?"

"I do not." He returned the ring to Ty. "And Nonna insists on it."

Lucia eye-hopped from one man to the other. "I don't understand what's going on."

Ty released a slow breath. "I don't either, but I suggest we get this done before anything else happens."

The priest performed the ceremony in record time. At the appropriate moment, Ty slipped the ring on Lucia's finger. To her delight, it fit as though made for her. When it came time for her to do the same for Ty, she realized she didn't have a ring for him.

Gabe came to the rescue. "I thought you might need this," he said, handing her a plain gold band.

Minutes later, the priest blessed the union, then took a moment to sit beside Nonna and pray with her. Gabe gave Lucia a fierce hug and a few minutes later, he and the priest departed, though she noticed her brother shot Primo a curious look. Okay, so it wasn't just her.

Ty gave a subtle jerk of his head, indicating it was time for them to leave, as well. Without a word, she crossed to Primo's side and wrapped her arms around him. She didn't understand any of this. Not why Nonna would insist they marry and Primo act as though it were the worst idea, ever. But she'd hold fire until she learned all the facts. Releasing her grandfather, she leaned down and kissed her grandmother.

"Today is your wedding day, so you will celebrate." Primo announced. He leveled Ty with a hard look. "Tomorrow, we will talk."

"What will we be talking about?" her brand-new husband asked, his voice deceptively mild.

"I would know who you really are, Ty Masterson." Primo's mouth compressed. "And more, I would know how that ring came to be in your possession."

Ty stiffened. "I already told you how I came to have the ring."

"And I tell you, that is not possible. So. We will talk, you and I. We will talk and we will get to the bottom of my questions."

Ty's mouth compressed. "Fine. We'll talk. It's not going to change my answers or anything I've already told you."

Primo lifted his shoulders in a shrug. "We shall each speak frank words and the truth will come. *Non avere peli sulla lingua.*"

Ty just shook his head at the bizarre slang directive, to have no hair on his tongue. He'd only heard it once before and understood it to mean they'd speak honestly with one another. Fair enough.

Crossing to Nonna's bed, he touched her shoulder. "We've done as you asked, Nonna. Lucia and I are married. Now you must do your part. Please fight to get better. Our children need to know their great-grandmother."

He turned and took Lucia's hand and drew her from the room. She shot a final look over her shoulder and he couldn't help but wonder if it would be her last glimpse of her grandmother. With a soft sigh, she turned away and walked hand-in-hand with Ty out of the ICU. He didn't say a word until they exited the hospital and were waiting for a cab.

"Okay, what was that all about?" His question sounded terse and vaguely offended. "What the hell did Primo mean, he wants to know who I really am?"

"I guess we'll find out tomorrow," she offered.

True. That didn't mean he had to like the delay. Setting the issue aside, Ty glanced down at her. "You do realize it's our wedding night?"

She fought back a smile. "Why, yes. It is."

"You're Mrs. Masterson now."

"Why, yes. I am."

He relaxed enough to chuckle. "We have a small problem."

"Where are we spending the night, tonight?" she asked.

He sighed. "That."

She gave it a moment's thought. "Would you mind if we just crash at your place? I feel like someone has beaten me from head to toe with a big stick. All I want to do is make love, take a long, hot shower, make love, sleep the clock around, and—"

"Make love?"

She slanted him a swift, teasing look. "That."

A cab pulled up and Ty helped her in. He rattled off the address and settled back against the seat, wrapping an arm around his wife. "So there's a slight catch if we spend the night at my place."

"I'm afraid to ask."

"I don't think Joe's available to cook for us. We won't starve. I'm pretty sure I have a jar of peanut butter somewhere."

"Pizza it is."

He lifted an eyebrow. "What? You don't like peanut butter?"

She snuggled close. "I gather you do?"

"Confession time. I have a serious love affair with peanut butter. I think it was because my mother never let me eat it. For years she told me I would die if I ate peanuts or peanut butter. The only time she ever hit me was when she caught me sneaking some."

"Were you okay?" she asked in concern.

"As it turned out, I was fine. She rushed me to the hospital, sure I'd go into anaphylaxis and stop breathing at any moment. I didn't, though even the doctors were surprised the allergy had gone away. Apparently, that doesn't happen very often."

"Are you sure you really had an allergy?"

"According to the doctors, I did. She had to call for an ambulance once before after I ate peanut butter. I don't recall the incident. I gather I was pretty little. I have to say, I'm glad I grew out of it. I don't think they'd have let me into the military, otherwise."

They pulled up in front of his house and, after paying the driver, Ty swept her into his arms and carried her over the threshold. Once inside with the door bolted behind them, he kissed her, a distinct melding of physical and emotional and spiritual. It was as though neither could get enough of the other.

Even when they resurfaced, it took a moment before he could speak. "Did you notice the priest didn't say I could kiss the bride?"

Lucia seemed to have a similar problem forming coherent words. "I think he was so rattled by Primo, he forgot about half the ceremony."

"I did notice a certain lack. He skipped right over the 'promise to obey' part."

She gave a delicate snort. "Good thing, since I'd have changed the wording."

He brows pulled together. "Is that legal?"

"I'm not even sure our marriage was legal. Did you give the priest the license? Did Gabe and Primo sign as witnesses?"

"Shit!"

She grimaced. "Yeah, that should have been done. Then Father Benito has to send it in. I think there's some sort of time limit."

"I'll get it to him in the morning."

"So, Primo is right? Our marriage didn't take?"

He drew a deep breath and blew it out. "Right now, all that matters is whether Nonna believed it."

Safe within his hold, Lucia tilted her head back and smiled up at him. "Thank you for being so sweet to her. I loved what you said."

"Honey, I meant every word," he said in all seriousness. "If our marriage helps her fight to get better, I couldn't ask for a better wedding gift."

She blinked away tears. "And Primo?"

"Count on it, we will get to the bottom of everything tomorrow."

Lucia's brows pulled together. "Primo didn't mention my attending the meeting, just you. I'm coming, too?"

His mouth tightened. "You're definitely coming, too."

"You realize I have nothing to wear? Again." She glanced down at her clothes and sighed. "Honestly, I can't remember the last time I wore one of my own outfits."

"The Wrangler was towed. I doubt anyone thought to grab our stuff out of there beforehand."

"That's it," she announced, thoroughly exasperated. "We'll just have to go naked from now on. It'll be easier, don't you think?"

"Infinitely." He found the side zip on her ruined wedding dress and lowered it. "Starting now."

The bodice dropped away and Lucia stepped free of the pool of dirt-streaked cream silk. Beneath she wore a pair of panties, a garter, and stockings. Of course, the stockings were ripped beyond recognition and Ty sucked in his breath at the sight of her skinned knees.

She peered down at them and winced. "Haven't had knees this bad since I was six and fell off my bike."

"I'm sorry, sweetheart. It's all my fault. I wasn't gentle when I yanked you out of the Wrangler and threw you on the ground."

She stepped into his arms and gave him a hug. "I don't think either of us were worried about gentle right at that moment. I think our main focus was on staying alive."

"True." He lifted her chin and planted a kiss on the tip of her nose. "Would you prefer a shower or a bath?"

"You have a bathtub?" she demanded, beyond thrilled.

"Sure."

Her eyes narrowed. "A big one?"

"A garden tub."

"A big one. Score!" She danced in place, then grabbed his hand and tugged. "Come on Tarzan, let's see how you handle bubbles."

"I didn't say I had bubbles, just a garden tub."

Her face fell and he laughed. "I have bubbles."

That stopped her for a moment. "You have bubbles. *You?*"

"Hey, even Tarzan can enjoy the occasional bubble bath."

She eyed him closely, attempting to ascertain whether or not he was serious. "Nah. You're yanking my chain."

He grinned. "I'm yanking your chain. I've never taken a bubble bath in my life." He waited a beat before adding, "But I do have bubbles."

She could think of just one explanation for that. A previous relationship. She released a drawn-out sigh. "Should I ask?"

"No."

"How long did it last?"

"Not long and far too long."

Hmm. Good answer. "Should I feel weird using her bubbles?"

He shrugged. "I don't know why you would. She didn't buy them. I did. Granted, she asked me to, but the relationship ended before any bubbling took place."

"In that case, let's go."

He swept her into his arms. Again. Should she tell him how much she loved his going all Tarzan on her? How much she appreciated his strength and the endless bulge of muscles? Not to mention, how protected she felt. After today, he'd officially become her real-life hero.

She rested her head against his shoulder, reveling in the strong, urgent beat of his heart and the ease with which he moved. He walked through a second bedroom, almost as large as the master, and into the attached, private bathroom. The tub took up an entire corner and featured a leaded glass window. Lights glittered through the thick colored panes. Fortunately, the fact that she couldn't see out, insured no one on the outside could see in.

He sat on the broad lip of the tub and started up the water, dumping a mound of the foaming bath salts under the sleek waterfall pouring from the faucet. Purple bubbles erupted, filling the room with the scent of lavender.

She scooped up a handful of bubbles and sniffed. "Perfect. Lavender helps you sleep."

He instantly frowned. "I don't want to sleep. I want to make love to my wife."

Oops. "Lavender also gives you a hard-on a horse would envy and the endurance of a bull," she immediately lied.

"You know far more about the sexual exploits of the animal kingdom than I do." He cocked an eyebrow. "Should I be concerned?"

"Only if a horse or bull joins us in the tub."

"I'll lock the door."

He set her on her feet and stripped away the remnants of her stockings, her garter, and finally her panties. She stood between his legs, feeling ever so slightly vulnerable, although she couldn't quite pinpoint why.

Then it struck her.

"What do you suppose Primo meant when he said our marriage wouldn't take?"

"Another issue we'll resolve when we see him tomorrow."

He stood, towering over her, and calmly undressed, tossing his wedding clothes onto the floor with careless disregard. Considering how ripped they were, she doubted they could be repaired. No point in worrying about a few wrinkles at this stage.

Naked, he stepped into the tub and helped her climb in. He sat and she slowly inched her way into the water, hissing when the soap suds licked across her various scrapes and cuts.

He gave her a sympathetic look. "Stings?"

"I don't think I realized how much until right now. And I'm so sore. I think my bruises have bruises." She spared him an annoyed grimace. "Why aren't you moaning and groaning?"

"I'm Tarzan, remember? Tarzan doesn't moan, let alone groan."

"Just points and grunts?"

"You got it."

He pointed to a spot in front of him and grunted. Pulling her down, he tucked her in front of him. She promptly sank beneath a mound of bubbles. With a chuckle he helped her resurface and settled her on his lap.

"I forget how tiny you are."

"I'm not tiny. I actually have way too many curves for a woman my size."

He snorted. "You realize there isn't a male in existence who believes that, right?"

"Wait one darn minute." She smacked the surface of the water, bubbles exploding around them. "Do I understand correctly that men like big breasts on a woman? Why has this been kept a secret?"

"Big breasts, nice round ass, and hips I can get a good grip on while we—"

She fought to suppress a laugh. "Yes, I get the picture, thank you."

He sobered. "Is that something else your ex gave you a hard time about?"

She closed her eyes and leaned back against him. "Yeah."

"You do realize there was something seriously wrong with him, right?"

She nodded. "I realize it now more than ever. That is one messed up family."

"Tell me that there aren't any more Benedicts."

"A mother and a sister. I'd worry about the sister except her two brothers spent their entire lives terrorizing her. I don't think she'll come gunning for me. She fell off the radar right before I divorced Andrew. Her mother said she planned to change her name and disappear."

"Sounds like she's the smart one in the family."

She swiveled around to face him, curling up against his bulk. "Let's not talk about them. Not tonight of all nights."

He hesitated a moment, then asked, "You want to talk about why Primo said our marriage wouldn't take?"

She shook her head. "I thought I did. I've changed my mind."

A slow, sensuous smile built across his handsome face. "What do you want to talk about?"

"I want to make sure you don't regret our marriage."

"His comment rattled you." He didn't phrase it as a question.

She nodded. "I've worked for my grandfather for a year now. I've gotten to know him really well. He's not someone who speaks without thinking. And what he does say, he means."

"Then we'll just have to prove him wrong, won't we?"

She took a deep breath and leveled him with an urgent, assessing gaze. "Is that what you want? To prove him wrong?"

"Don't you?"

She settled the palms of her hands against his chest, The Inferno singing through her. She shivered in reaction, wondering how she'd possibly handle it if their marriage didn't "take." She couldn't. It was that simple.

"You know what I'm asking, Ty. If it weren't for Nonna we wouldn't have married so quickly. I mean, we've only known each other for days. The speed of our marriage . . . Well, quite frankly, it's crazy."

He took the observation in stride. "I can't argue with that. And, I have to be honest, I keep expecting to wake up and want out."

"You did after our first date," she dared to mention.

He nodded. "For good reason."

She flipped her hand over so the odd tattoo faced upward. "I don't disagree." She traced the lovely swirl she'd come to treasure, perhaps because it emblemized The Inferno. "None of this makes the least bit of sense."

"And yet, here we sit in a tub full of bubbles," he teased. "Married. After only knowing each other a handful of days."

Lucia sighed. "I have it on good authority that's par for the course with The Inferno."

Ty ran his thumb across the mark decorating her palm, smiling at her helpless shiver. "He recognized this mark."

"I know." Her brows drew together. "Do you suppose that's why he was so upset?"

Ty tilted his head to one side in consideration, taking his time before answering. "I had the impression the mark surprised him, but it didn't upset him. It's the ring that upset him."

Lucia gazed at the lovely confection of gold and diamonds decorating her hand. It was absolutely beautiful. And somehow familiar. Now that she really looked at it, *very* familiar. Where had she seen it before?

A memory teased at her. Before she could make the connection, Ty hooked her chin and lifted her face to his. "Enough. We've allowed far too many ghosts to haunt us today. Let's end this evening with just the two of us."

She snuggled close. "And some pizza."

"And some pizza. But first . . ."

He lifted her slightly, opening her to him. She moaned softly, swiveling her hips so she straddled his impressive erection, slowly easing down onto it. It speared into her, filling her. Stretching her. Scraping inward and hitting the perfect spot.

"Just like that," she whispered.

He thrust upward just as she rocked downward and pleasure ripped through her. He wrapped her tight against him, moving slow and cautiously, water swirling around them. The bubbles teased her skin, bursting in little arousing explosions.

Ty moved faster. Harder. The water sloshed, threatening to spill over the rim of the tub and onto the tile floor. "Come on, sweetheart. You're in control. Take me where you want to go."

Her breasts slid across his chest with every movement, piling sensation on top of sensation. It wasn't enough. She needed more. As though picking up on her thoughts, he slid his hands into her hair and lifted her face to his. His mouth closed over hers, hard and demanding, devouring her with urgent sweeps of his tongue. He caught her lower lip between his teeth and tugged.

Grabbing her hips, he helped her move, pistoning faster, driving into her. It was too much. Too much raw emotion. Too many confusing events stacked one on the other in a haphazard jumble. With a cry, she tumbled. His hoarse shout joined hers, echoing around the bathroom. Gasping for breath, she collapsed against him.

Neither of them moved for several long minutes. "I never knew hurt and satisfaction could go together like that," she murmured.

His laughter rumbled against her ear. "Has the warm water helped at all?"

"I don't know. Find my body and ask it."

He peered over the edge of the tub. "We soaked the bathroom floor."

"The maid will clean it up."

"We have a maid?" For some reason that made her laugh. Bizarrely, it sounded a lot like tears. Ty must have thought the same. "Shh. It's okay. Everything is going to work out, I promise."

"You promised me pizza," she wept. "Why aren't I eating pizza?"

He pushed her hair away from her face. "Are you crying because you're hungry? Or are you sad? Or has everything that's happened today finally hit?"

"Yes," she managed to get out around a sob.

"Got it." He grunted, a hint of pain running through the sound. Apparently, he hadn't escaped without a number of bruises, either. "Up we go."

Lucia slipped her way to her feet and they climbed out of the tub, dripping water and bubbles all over the bathmat. Ty crossed to a linen closet and pulled out a stack of towels. Half of them he flung onto the floor. The other half he flung over the two of them.

"What do you say we order that pizza?"

She sniffed. "Okay. What kind?"

"Hell, woman. There's only one kind of pizza."

She sighed. *So* like Gabe. "Pepperoni it is."

"Thank God." He shot her a stern look. "For a minute there, I was afraid Primo was right."

Laughter replaced her tears. "You'd divorce me over pizza?"

"Hell, yes, I'd divorce you over pizza." He eyed her with open suspicion. "If you have any similar issues, maybe you'd better get them into the open now. Anything I need to do or not do, eat or not eat, say or not say?"

She considered. "Don't lie to me. The only good anchovy is a dead one, well blended into a Cesar salad dressing, otherwise I don't want to see or smell it." She hesitated, not certain she should admit this next part.

"Spill it, sweetcakes."

"You're going to have to rethink the whole sweetcakes thing." She darted a nervous glance upward. "Other than that, when you're ready and when it's right and when you're sure, I wouldn't mind hearing the L word."

"Got it."

"But not until you're sure and it's real."

"Fair enough. Ditto."

Her mouth trembled into a smile at another *Ghost* reference. It was the perfect thing to say. "Food."

"I'm on it."

Since she didn't have anything to wear, she scurried to his bedroom—*their* bedroom now—and raided his closet. She frowned, rifling through the shirts neatly hanging there. Did the man own any color other than black? She squinted. Okay, navy, though she didn't think that counted as a different color. Maybe she should introduce him to the concept of a color wheel. Or did that fall into the same category as a Hawaiian pizza? Choosing a black shirt, she climbed into it, not the least surprised to discover it hung to her knees.

After swiping Ty's comb, Lucia crossed to the living room, spotting him by the liquor cabinet. Instantly, his head swiveled in her direction. The drink he'd been pouring overflowed the tumbler and he swore, fumbling with both decanter and glass. "Hey, don't do that to me."

She blinked in confusion. "I'm sorry? Do what?"

He made an up and down gesture. "You know. Look like that."

She glanced down at herself and buried a smile, warmth flooding through her. Apparently, he liked how she looked in his shirt. Or maybe he liked what she had under it, which was nothing.

"Should I take it off?" she asked in mock innocence.

"Would you?"

A laugh bubbled free. "No. At least, not now."

Heat flared in his black gaze. "In that case, I look forward to later."

"I'm beginning to think I married an insatiable man."

He crossed the room and offered her a drink. "The real question is, did I marry an insatiable woman?"

"If you'd asked me that when we first met, I'd have said no. I've never wanted anyone before, not the way I want you." She shrugged helplessly. "I don't understand."

"You don't need to understand it." He clinked his glass against hers. "*Per cent'anni!*"

"What does that mean?"

"Literally, for a hundred years. But the toast is actually saying, may we live for a hundred years."

"That's lovely."

"So are you." He gestured toward the couch. "Pizza is on its way. We have a nice, blazing fire going. We each have a drink. Let's just relax."

Last time she'd been here, they'd sat on opposite ends of the cushioned length. This time, they curled up like two halves of a whole. Held safe within his arms, she'd never felt so snug and warm. "Thank you," she murmured. "This is perfect."

He took the comb from her and settled her head on his lap, then gently worked at the endless tangles. "I see this will be a full-time job."

"Sure you're up for it?" she asked around a yawn.

"I'll manage."

She struggled to keep her eyes open, his soothing touch turning her bones liquid. The day had been one of endless highs and lows with no time to catch her breath in between. Exhaustion rippled through her and she yawned again. She barely noticed when he slipped her glass from her hand and set it on the end table closest to him.

What had Primo meant? Why would their marriage not take? Didn't he understand how she felt about Ty? How perfect they were together? Didn't The Inferno mean they were destined to spend the rest of their lives together? Nonna had seemed to think so or she wouldn't have insisted they marry.

Well, she didn't care what Primo thought. Their marriage might have been precipitous, but that didn't mean it couldn't work out, especially considering how she felt about Ty.

"Did you say something?" he asked.

"Mmm." Her eyes drifted shut and words filled her head and heart, words she clutched close and drew comfort from. Words she didn't dare speak, except to herself. "I love you, Ty. I've loved you from the moment we first met. And I'll love you until the moment we part. And even then, I'll still love you."

Maybe someday she could tell him that, came her final thought. And then sleep claimed her.

Chapter Ten

Ty woke his wife with a tender kiss to her forehead. She stirred, murmuring a small protest. "I hate to do this to you, but you need to get up."

She opened a single, blurry eye. It was not a happy eye. "You should run."

"Yup. A smart man would. Sadly, you aren't married to a smart man." He tossed back the covers and pulled her upright. God, she was beautiful, even grouchy. "I let you sleep as long as I could, but we need to find something for you to wear, and then drive to Dantes. We're supposed to meet Primo in less than an hour."

"How's Nonna?" she instantly asked.

"I haven't heard anything. I'm assuming that's good news."

"Wait." She glared at him. "What happened to my pizza?"

"You slept through it."

"Why didn't you wake me?"

"You slept through my waking you."

"You ate my pizza?" she demanded, outraged.

"No, I ate *my* pizza." He rubbed his jaw in thought. "Now that I think about it, I might have eaten yours, too. Lucky for you I anticipated that possibility and ordered two pizzas. The extra one is warming in the oven."

"Wait. Pizza for breakfast?" She catapulted into his arms, lacing her hands around his neck and her legs around his waist. "You are the best husband *ever* and it's only the first day of our marriage. Or is it the second?"

"Shall we settle for the first twenty-four hours of marriage?"

"It's a deal." She planted a swift kiss on his cheek. "I'd give you a better kiss, but you know. Morning breath."

"I'll chance it."

Might as well start the way he intended to go on. He kissed her long and hard and deep. She melted against him, her response both passionate and uninhibited. Did she mean the words she'd whispered last night? Had she really fallen in love with him? Could love happen so quickly?

Why did he ask such a ridiculous question, considering how he felt about her?

Maybe The Inferno accelerated everything, punching the fast-forward button on what might have taken months under normal conditions? He shook his head in amusement.

"What?" she demanded. "What's so funny?"

"I was thinking about The Inferno."

She eyed him warily. "There's something funny about The Inferno?"

"No, there's something funny about my even considering the possibility The Inferno exists." He lowered her to her feet. "You've got to be starving. I don't think you've had anything to eat since breakfast yesterday."

"You're right. I haven't."

She made a beeline for the kitchen, shoving at the sleeves of his shirt that dangled from her fingertips. She picked up the hot pads beside the oven and Ty stepped in, stopping her before she could open the door.

"Let me do that for you. I think we've ruined enough clothes. I'd rather not scorch my shirt, too."

"Okay." She crossed to the table tucked into the bay window and took a seat, planting one foot on the edge of the chair and wrapping her arms around her bent knee. "So, you're an Inferno believer now, huh?"

He removed the pizza tray from the oven and placed it on top of the stove. "I'm not sure I'd take it that far." In a single deft movement, he transferred the pizza from the tray to a serving platter and carried it to the table, setting it between them. "Let's say, I'm willing to discuss it, but I have serious doubts. Coffee or Coke?"

"You can't drink coffee when you're eating pizza."

"Coke, it is."

"Weirdest breakfast I've had in a long time, but I think it might become one of my favorites," she confessed.

"Actually, I can't say the same."

She waved a floppy sleeve in his direction. "You can't stop there. Spill."

"Let's see. A cold MRE of beef ravioli. I think that cheese spread is still glued to my guts." He grabbed a slice of pizza, folded it in half and chowed down. "A fairly common option was a bowl of milk and dates, called *sheer khurma*. That one was pretty good. Better than an MRE."

"Meals Ready to Eat?"

"You got it."

"I think I'll stick with pizza."

They ate in companionable silence for the rest of their breakfast. Satisfied, Lucia sat back and studied her palm, stroking the pretty swirl centered there. "I want to ask Primo about these marks. He definitely knows more about them than he's telling us."

"And I want to know what the deal is with my father's ring. Not to mention the small matter of whether or not our marriage has taken."

"Well, the only way we're going to find out is if we meet with him. The sooner the better."

The doorbell rang just then and Ty excused himself to answer it. A minute later, he returned with a shopping bag. He held it aloft. "As much as I prefer you either naked or wearing one of my shirts, you now have clothes again. Let's try not to ruin these."

She stood and took the bag from him. "I'll go change. I should be ready to go in just a sec." She snapped her fingers and turned back toward him. "Hey, we should get that marriage license taken care of after we see Primo."

"Already done. I took care of it first thing this morning while you were sleeping."

Relief flooded through her. How did she get so lucky? "Wow, you've been busy. Thanks."

"You're welcome."

Less than thirty minutes later, they arrived at the corporate headquarters of Dantes and took the elevator to the executive floor. Lucia led the way to Primo's office and found him waiting for them, a wreath of cigar smoke encircling his head.

She crossed to her grandfather's side and gave him a quick hug and kiss. "How's Nonna?"

"Your marriage, it has helped her," he admitted with a broad smile. "She is more herself today. Sev and Lazz are with her this morning."

Lucia beamed, relief washing across her expression. "That's great news." Then her smile faded. "I think we have a lot to talk about, though, don't we?"

"We do, child. Sit, sit." For the first time, he turned to face Ty, who waited to see what sort of reception he'd receive. To his surprise, Primo offered his hand. "Where shall we start?"

He decided to have Primo address Lucia's question first. "You recognized the marks on our palms. How? Why?"

Primo took his time answering, releasing a fragrant puff of cigar smoke. "I have seen them before. Or ones similar to those."

"Where?" He fought to keep the question from sounding terse and failed miserably.

"On the palms of my Dante relatives. That is why I said you were not Ty Masterson." Primo stabbed the glowing tip of his cigar in Ty's direction. "You are a Dante."

Ty started to shake his head, then hesitated. Was it possible? His mother had never identified his father. Could he be a Dante?

"Wait," Lucia interrupted, alarm a stark undercurrent. She held her hands up. "Just wait a minute. *I'm* a Dante. At least, my father was. Are you saying Ty and I are *related?*"

"I am saying this, yes."

Lucia turned a wide, panicked gaze in Ty's direction and he glared at the old man. *"How* related?"

Primo thumped his index finger against his own chest. "If I am the trunk of my family tree," he gestured to the far recesses of the room, "there sits Ty's family tree. Those who dwell in your tree are cousins of my own *nonno.* You and Lucia are cousins separated by many branches. But both still Dantes."

Okay. That wasn't too bad. He reached for Lucia's hand and gripped it tightly. "So, we're distant cousins. An odd coincidence, but we shouldn't end up with three-eyed children."

Primo released a bark of laughter. "Not three-eyed children, no. But a double dose of The Inferno, yes."

"What do you mean?" Lucia asked. "What double dose?"

"Ah." He leaned back in his chair and closed his eyes, perhaps to gather his thoughts and organize them into a coherent whole. At long last he regarded them, a certain sadness lingering in the depths. Old memories haunted his gaze, clinging like ancient cobwebs. "My *nonno* once told me all Dantes are marked by The Inferno in some fashion. Some, like Lucia, feel its presence like a burn, an itch centered in the palm. Yes?"

Lucia nodded, rubbing the center of her palm. "Yes, just like that."

He nodded in Ty's direction. "Others, these cousins I mention, receive a mark. Whether mark or burn, it does not matter. The end result remains. When you touch your soul mate, The Inferno flares to life. My family is fortunate. We know then and there." He turned his attention to Ty. "Your family, not so fortunate. They must wait until the mark appears, then figure out who they touched. Who carries a mark that matches their own."

Ty lifted an eyebrow. "If we both have the mark, why does only Lucia feel the burn?"

Amusement glittered in his burnished gaze and he lifted a shoulder in a half shrug. "Who can say? The Inferno has not granted me this knowledge. Do you doubt The Inferno, the possibility that you and Lucia have experienced it?"

Ty gave the issue serious consideration. "I'd be lying if I said I believe without qualification," he admitted at last. "It sounds too bizarre to just accept without question."

Primo nodded. "This I can understand, though it does not change what has happened. The end result remains the same. If you are smart, you will heed the mark and your marriage will be blessed. But if you ignore it, if you turn from The Inferno out of fear or ignorance or stubbornness, that blessing becomes a curse."

"A curse," Ty repeated.

Primo shook his finger at him. It would have been amusing if not for the grave expression carved across the old man's face. "For the rest of your life you will live with regret. If you marry another, one who is not your Inferno mate, that marriage will be a disaster for you both. Hear my warning and heed it. Ignore The Inferno at your own peril. My own son ignored it and experienced its curse instead of its blessing. Lucia married out of ignorance and her marriage was another disaster."

Ty spared his wife a concerned look, relieved that she appeared to take the comment in stride. "Okay, then we're good, right? We're married, aren't we?"

"But are you united?"

"Primo!" Lucia reprimanded, turning red.

The old man released a roar of laughter. "The young are so repressed. Child, I did not mean sexual congress. I refer to your hearts and minds. Are they united? Or was this wedding ceremony just for Nonna's benefit?"

She released a sigh. "Maybe a little of both? What does it matter? We're married."

He hid behind a fog of cigar smoke. "Perhaps."

Ty chose to interrupt. "So, you think I'm related to these cousins of yours?"

"I do. Those Dantes, most of them dwell in Texas now. We call them Those Damn Texas Dantes because they are rude and cocky. It is possible those are your people."

Ty started to say something rude and cocky and caught himself at the last minute. "And you think my father stems from those Dantes?"

"Before I answer, I think it is now time for me to ask you questions, Mr. Ty Masterson who is not Ty Masterson."

He stirred in annoyance. "Why do you keep saying that?"

Primo waved his concern aside. "I have already said it is my turn to ask the questions. Then you may ask any which I have not already answered. The first question will be an easy one. Tell me your mother's name."

"Candice. Candice Masterson."

"I wish to know more about Candice. Not how you describe her to most people, but the truth you keep buried deep inside." He swept a hand from heart to head. "Here. And here. Tell me, was she good to you?"

"Yes."

Primo nodded. "This makes me glad." He pointed at Ty, moving his index finger in a slow circle. "But there is something I sense here. If you were to describe your *mamma,* what one word would you use?"

"Sad." The description escaped without thought or hesitation and the instant he said it, he longed to yank it back. He released a sigh. "She was often sad, especially around Christmas. Christmases were rough in our household."

Primo's golden eyes focused with hard, unrelenting determination. "Now I ask an odd question and you will give me an immediate and truthful answer. *Sei d'accordo?*"

"*Sono d'accordo.*"

"Were you ever in a train wreck?"

Ty inhaled sharply. "How did you know that?"

Primo closed his eyes, deep lines carving a path from cheekbone to the corners of his mouth. "Ah. That explains much."

Tension filled him. "Explains what?"

"I do not believe you are Ty Masterson," Primo shocked him by saying. "I believe your name is Romero Dante."

"Wait," Lucia interrupted. "That's *your* name."

"*Sì.* If your husband is who I believe, he was named in my honor." Sorrow filled his gaze. "That train wreck happened on Christmas Eve and took many lives. It took the life of a boy of four named Romero Dante, along with his parents. The train wreck, it occurred not far from Dallas. Would this be the same accident you were involved in?"

"Yes. I was also four." Ty swallowed. "But, if Romero died, then I can't be him."

Primo nodded. "Unless, it was not Romero who was killed that sad day, but the young son of the woman you called *mamma*. You describe her as sad, and admit it grew worse at Christmas. Perhaps it grew worse because Christmas marked the occasion of her true son's death. The real Ty Masterson's death. Based on what you know of her, is this at all possible?"

He clamped his back teeth together, his jaw clenching. "I couldn't say."

"Could not? Or will not?"

Ty's hands closed into fists, possibilities spinning through his head.

"I see you are putting together memories of your past and wondering if I am not correct," Primo said gently.

"Maybe," he gritted out.

Primo puffed on his cigar and gave Ty a moment to reflect before speaking again. "I wonder . . . I wonder if in the traumatic aftermath of this horrendous train wreck, upon seeing her only child dead, if Candice did not commit an act she would not normally think to commit. In her unbalanced state, did she claim you were her child? When she saw you lived and your parents did not, when she saw her own child taken from her, is it possible in that terrible instant she acted in a way contrary to her nature? Did she decide she could not live without her child and you became that child for her?"

"You're reaching," Ty snapped.

Primo held up his hands. "Possibly. Possibly. Still, I wonder." He leaned forward, intensity slipping through his words and across his face. "Did Candice Masterson somehow convince herself you were hers and over the years came to believe it? This sadness you speak of... Perhaps when reality intruded upon fantasy and the truth could no longer be denied, such as the anniversary of the accident, the anniversary of her true son's death, she struggled to face what she'd done. It would explain her sadness."

"Or maybe she just didn't like Christmas."

"Or maybe her guilt and grief became too much to bear. Maybe the truth haunted her at that time of year."

Damn it to hell! Ty looked away, Primo's words hammering relentlessly at his heart and soul. It would explain so much about his mother, his childhood, the odd things she would say at times. Her rushing him to the hospital after catching him eating peanut butter and her bizarre insistence that he was deathly allergic to it when he wasn't. Her spending every Christmas Eve in her room, weeping. The ring she gave him and her odd phrasing when describing it.

The ring belonged to your father.

Ty longed to deny the possibility that he wasn't who he'd always believed. Longed to offer proof he was Ty Masterson and not Romero Dante. One final incident stopped him. His mother's words on her deathbed.

I wish I really were your mother.

Lucia shifted in his direction, murmuring his name, her hand tightening around his in clear support. One glance warned she'd made a similar connection.

"And if it's possible?" he whispered hoarsely.

Compassion slid across Primo's face. "If you are willing, we can uncover the truth. There are tests."

"And if the test proves I'm not Romero Dante? If I really am Ty Masterson?"

"Then your father is a Dante. There is no other explanation for why you bear that mark upon your palm, one you share with my Lucia. It comes from The Inferno and is unique to the Dante line." Primo's eyes turned cold and hard. "However, that does not explain the ring you gave to my *nipote*. And that brings us to the final part of our conversation today."

Ty stiffened. "What are you talking about?"

"This ring, it never belonged to your mother. She stole it."

It took every ounce of self-possession to remain seated and not lose his shit completely. "I suggest you explain that accusation and fast."

"This ring was made for the couple who died in that train wreck. It disappeared on that day and has not been seen again until yesterday, when you pulled it from beneath your shirt."

No. No way. He fought to remain seated, to remain calm. Never had he worked so hard to achieve so little. "How could you possibly know?" he ground out.

Primo held him with his golden gaze, his words thick with the lyricism of his homeland. "I know because I created that ring. Designed that ring. Made that ring with my own two hands. I gave the ring to Silvio and Emilia Dante as a gift to honor their union. My cousins and I had a parting of ways before I left Italy many decades before. The ring was reparations, of a sort."

Ty swore beneath his breath and a cold sweat trickled down his back. Dear God, could Primo be right? Could his entire life have been based on a lie? "Is there any other possibility?"

"I can think of none." Primo leaned back and gestured with his cigar. "Perhaps once you have had time to reflect, an alternate possibility may occur to you. In my opinion, the only way your mother could possess the ring is if she took it or found it after the wreck that day."

"She wasn't a thief," he objected.

"Under normal circumstances, no. But I suspect she took you, which was a theft. And if she gave you that ring, then she must have taken that, as well." He looked away briefly, struggling against the emotions gripping him. At long last, he turned back, his eyes like tarnished gold and filled with grief. "I try to look at the situation as my Nonna would, with compassion. I will offer this possibility . . . Perhaps Candice Masterson took the ring so you would have something that belonged to your true parents. She could not tell you the ring belonged to your *mamma* when she claimed to be that mother. So she told you it came from your father, which is a version of the truth."

"And you're sure it's the same ring?"

"I am. I can even prove it. *Nipote,* if you will give me the ring?" Without a word, Lucia tugged it off her finger and passed it to her grandfather. "I am surprised you did not recognize it."

It took her a second, but then she gave a soft gasp, shooting Ty an apologetic glance. "I thought it looked familiar. You've shown me pictures of it, haven't you?"

"I have."

Using his thumb nail, he split apart the ring, revealing how it was actually two pieces seamlessly joined into one. He picked up a book resting on the corner of the desk, no doubt in anticipation of this part of their conversation. He flipped it open to a marked page featuring a large color photograph and turned it toward Ty. He set the two parts of the ring on top of the picture.

Ty stood and gazed down at the book. Sure enough, the photo was identical to the ring his mother had given him. In all the years she'd had it, she'd never shown him how the ring could be separated into a combination of a wedding band and an engagement ring. Did she even know? He peered closer.

"It's inscribed."

"*Forever Dante.* Words of unity. Words meant to bring two fractured families together again." He spared Lucia a loving glance. "It is an appropriate ring for you, child. For you have always been a Dante, no matter how hard you have fought it in recent years. And now, once we have straightened out Ty's true identity, you will always carry that name. Forever Dante."

Ty flinched. No. He was a Masterson, not a Dante. He'd been a Masterson for thirty-five years. He couldn't just become something he wasn't. Was. Maybe was.

What. The. *Hell!*

He'd never dealt with such a bizarre situation. Everything he thought he knew about himself might be a lie. How did he square with that? Gently, he picked up the two parts of the ring and carefully clicked them together into a single, seamless piece. And just like that, his thoughts solidified.

Either he'd been born a Masterson or a Dante. He needed to know which. Because until he did, he wouldn't feel settled. Wouldn't feel as though he belonged to either world. He'd remain on the outside, looking in, living in limbo, a place he knew well. And once he knew the truth?

He'd deal with it. He'd click into place, like the ring.

He released a slow breath. "Even the way the two parts join is symbolic, isn't it?"

Primo shot him a pleased look. "Exactly. Though they are two, when linked together, it is almost impossible to see where one begins and the other ends. So should be your marriage. Two separate parts become one, the union so complete, they form an unbreakable whole."

Ty turned and took Lucia's hands in his. This time when he placed it on her finger, he realized it felt different. *He* felt different. Did Lucia? He flashed her a swift, concerned look. It suddenly occurred to him that if he were, in fact, Romero Dante and not Ty Masterson, there might be issues with their marriage. His gaze slid to Primo and he saw calm understanding reflected there.

"That's what you meant," he accused. "When you said this marriage wouldn't take."

Primo inclined his head. "That is what I meant."

"Then why did you let us go through with it?"

He shrugged his broad shoulders. "What if I am wrong? You had already taken my Lucia to your bed." He made a shushing motion in her direction, his gaze locked with Ty's. "Better you marry, even if it must be undone and done again. For now, you are Ty Masterson. For now, you and Lucia are legally wed. *Quel che sarà.*"

"Easy for you to say."

Primo waved that aside with a brief, *"Basta."* He turned his attention to Lucia. "You will visit your Nonna tomorrow."

He didn't phrase it as a request and she didn't take it that way. "Of course."

He returned his attention to Ty. "And Mr. not-Ty Masterson. You agree to take the test to see who you truly are?"

He'd never been the sort to stick his head in the sand. Besides, he wanted to know the truth. "Yes, I'll take the test."

"I will make the arrangements." He stood and they followed suit. "It is time for me to return to my Nonna. I have been too long from her side. My office is yours. Stay and talk through what has been said. This cannot be an easy day for you."

Ty remained silent until Primo left the office. He turned to Lucia, who instantly stepped into his arms. "Are you okay?" she asked.

He released a harsh laugh. "No, not really."

"All of this must have come as quite a shock."

"You could say that."

She pulled back slightly. "What are you going to do if you find out you're really Romero Dante?"

He shook his head. "I have no idea. I still can't wrap my head around Primo's claims." He hesitated, then confessed in a low voice, "But I think he's right. It . . . clicked, like the ring. Fit together in a way that made sense."

"And it explains your mother's final words to you." Her arms tightened around him. "I'm sorry. I know how it feels when you learn things about your parents that are difficult to accept."

He kissed the top of her head. "I know you do."

"I can't help wondering how Primo's revelation will affect our marriage."

He'd already wondered the same, though he didn't say anything. "Let's just take it one step at a time."

"We seem to be saying that a lot over the past few days. Have you noticed that each step we take makes our lives more and more complicated?"

"Why, no, I hadn't noticed."

A helpless laugh escaped at his teasing sarcasm. She took a deep breath and nodded. "Okay. Okay, one step at a time, one day at a time."

Not that it would change anything. He swiftly considered options and analyzed them, an occupational hazard. Some were worth further consideration, others he dismissed out-of-hand. Unfortunately, the one he liked least struck him as the most honorable.

When the time came, if their marriage was thrown into doubt, he'd give Lucia an out if she wished to take it. An out of their marriage and an out of his life. Only one problem with that plan.

She'd never be out of his heart.

Chapter Eleven

The next two weeks slid by. At times it seemed to Lucia as though it moved at warp speed and at others it crawled along, frame by frame in slow-motion. Nonna continued to cling to life, though the doctors offered little encouragement, and each day rested on a knife's edge, teetering between possibility and disaster.

She and Ty also teetered between possibility and disaster, either making love with a frantic desperation or tiptoeing around issues better left unspoken. Issues such as his identity and their marriage, not to mention their plans for the future. Perhaps they'd have lasted in limbo, if Nonna hadn't once again interceded, requesting Lucia visit her at the hospital.

To Lucia's surprise she discovered her grandmother all alone. "I asked the others to give us some time together," Nonna explained.

"Is something wrong?"

A faint smile touched her grandmother's mouth. "You mean beside the obvious?"

Lucia winced. "I'm sorry."

"Do not be sorry, child. All will happen as it is meant to." She gathered Lucia's hand in hers. For a long moment, she closed her eyes, causing Lucia to wonder if she'd fallen asleep. Then her lashes fluttered and she drew in a deep breath. "Tell me the truth, my sweet girl. Have you and Ty accepted one another? Have you both accepted The Inferno and your Dante roots? Or do you still fight what is . . . what must be?"

Lucia hesitated. Should she be honest? It seemed such a heavy burden to place on such weak shoulders. Even so, she couldn't bring herself to lie. "I can feel Ty pulling away," she confessed.

"And why is this?"

She shook her head. "I don't know. It's almost as though he's bracing himself. As though he expects something to happen that will separate us."

Nonna nodded. "You confirm what I suspected. He is afraid, *nipote.*"

"Ty?"

The thought struck her as laughable. He was the strongest, most confident and self-assured person she'd ever met. He'd shown unbelievable courage in the face of unfathomable danger. Ty, afraid? No way.

"You must find out why he pulls away and what he fears. If you do this, all will be resolved." Once again, Nonna closed her eyes, gathering her fading strength. "Have you told him?"

The change in subject caught Lucia off guard. "Told him what?"

"That you are pregnant."

Time hitched, missing a beat. All Lucia could do was stare at her grandmother. "What?"

Nonna's lips curved into a smile. "A girl. I did not see this until just recently. She will be a fae child."

"What?" Lucia repeated, struggling to keep her voice calm and level, and failing miserably.

Nonna's voice turned dreamy. "She will have the eye, as I do, able to see what others cannot. And she will be a tiny sprite of a child, one foot here and one foot in a place few can see. And beautiful. So beautiful. She will be the loveliest of all my great-grandchildren."

Lucia shook her head in disbelief. "You can't possibly know that. Ty and I have only been together—"

"Long enough to create a child." Her grandmother's eyes fluttered closed and her breath grew faint. "You must leave me, my darling girl. You must fix things with Ty. Now. Before the window closes."

"Nonna, are you all right?" Lucia shot to her feet. "Do you need the doctor?"

"I just need my Primo," she whispered. "I need him now. Quickly, Lucia."

Without a word, Lucia flew from the cubicle. She waved down a nurse. "Something's wrong with my grandmother. Julietta Dante."

The nurse didn't take the time to respond, simply made a beeline toward Nonna's cubicle. Lucia rushed from the ICU and darted into the waiting room. Primo sat with Luc in quiet conversation. "Nonna is asking for you, Primo. Something's wrong."

Without a word, he stood, his cane clutched tight in his pawlike grip. Luc accompanied him through the doors into the ICU unit. Tears burned in her eyes. She'd known since the shooting that Nonna might not make it. Known how hard her grandmother had struggled. *Please, don't give up,* she silently prayed. *Please don't die.*

To her profound relief, Luc returned a few minutes later, though his report wasn't encouraging. "She's resting. They think she's losing blood and needs more surgery."

Alarm shot through her. "Can she handle more surgery?"

Luc simply shook his head. "I'm not sure they have any choice. She won't survive without it." He didn't add the alternative. She might not survive another procedure, either. He gave her a swift hug. "There's nothing you can do here, Lucia. If they operate, it won't be until later today or tomorrow. Go on home. We'll keep you updated."

She hated to leave, but didn't see much point in remaining. If Nonna was right about Ty—and more importantly—right about a pregnancy, she needed to have a serious talk with her husband. But even before that, she needed to pick up a pregnancy kit that would either confirm or refute Nonna's suspicions. She stopped at a drug store on her way home and purchased the most accurate test on the market before returning to Ty's house—now their home.

The second she stepped inside, she could tell he hadn't returned from his appointment with the police. The house felt too quiet and empty. Clearly, finalizing details regarding the investigation into Orrin Benedict's death was taking longer than anticipated. On the plus side, that gave her the opportunity to take the pregnancy test before his return.

It only took five short minutes to confirm part of Nonna's claim. The two pink lines indicating a positive pregnancy couldn't be any brighter or more clearly delineated. She stared for endless moments at the results, filled with a bizarre combination of excitement and worry.

She rested her hand over her lower abdomen, stunned to realize she carried a tiny life there. A girl, if Nonna's eye was as accurate as everyone claimed. A daughter who might very well be the product of two Dante lines. A strange possessiveness swept through her, a primal instinct to protect and nurture the baby she carried.

How would Ty react when she told him? Would he experience that same instinct? She knew the answer before it even fully formed. She'd never met a more protective man in her entire life. That left only one small problem . . .

Would he feel obligated to stay married to her? Because she didn't want to force him to remain in a marriage unless he loved her. And so far, he hadn't said the words.

The bang of the front door brought her back to the present and she hurried through the bedroom to the living room. Ty stood there, and it didn't take more than a single look to realize something had gone seriously wrong. He stalked toward her, yanking off his clothes as he came and discarding them along the way. Reaching her, he snagged her around the waist and dragged her in for a long, hard kiss.

"You aren't naked," he growled the complaint.

Those were all the words he spoke for the next thirty minutes. He had her clothes stripped away even faster than his own. They didn't even make it to the bedroom, but ended up on the floor in a frantic tangle of arms and legs. He made love to her with an urgency edged with desperation, as though it were the last time they'd ever be together again. And part of her wondered if that weren't the truth.

At long last, they collapsed into an exhausted heap, struggling to draw breath. "What was all that about?" she dared to ask, gasping for air. "Not that I'm complaining."

"Ty Masterson is dead."

She jerked upright, twisting to stare down at him. "The DNA test came back?"

"You're married to Romero Dante. Or is it, not married?" He draped an arm across his face. "Shit."

"Ty, look at me."

He released a harsh laugh, moving his arm just enough to glare up at her. "Didn't you hear me? I'm not Ty."

Oh, God. No question the results had hit him hard. "It's not your name that defines you, sweetheart," she told him gently. "Ty Masterson is just a name, like Moretti or Benedict. Or Romero Dante. You can choose what people call you. That's entirely up to you. But a name doesn't change who you are inside."

"It was all a lie, Lucia. My mother . . ." He swore again. "Only, she's not my mother, is she? I don't even know what to call her."

Her heart broke for him. "She raised you. That makes her your mother, don't you think? How she ended up with you might have been wrong, a horrible wrong. But she loved you. She cared for you."

Her words seemed to calm him and he blew out his breath. "I'm angry."

"I get that." She cupped his face in a loving gesture. He turned into her hand, her Inferno hand, and planted a lingering kiss directly on top of the stylistic half-moon. "And you have every right to be angry."

"I'm glad you agree."

She ignored the hint of sarcasm. "You're still allowed to love her. You realize that, right?" She let that sink in for a moment before adding, "Because you do love her, don't you?"

He sat up and scraped his hands over his face. "Yeah." The admission seemed to ease the tension vibrating through him. "Yeah, I love her. Still love her. She was the only mother I can remember. And even if I wasn't the son she gave birth to, I think she came to love me as though I were. At least, that's what I choose to believe."

"Then focus on that." She climbed into his lap and wrapped her arms around his neck. "Listen, it's going to take time to deal with what's happened. You don't need to make any decisions right away about how to handle what you've learned. You don't even have to use the Dante name, if you don't want."

He kissed the sensitive curve at the juncture of her neck and shoulder. "And our marriage?"

She couldn't help stiffening. "What about it?"

His eyes were so dark, all emotion shuttered, locking her out. "I planned to do the honorable thing and let you go," he informed her.

Panic shot through her. Why was ending their marriage the honorable thing? Then she realized he'd used the past tense. "Planned?" she repeated. The fact that she managed to ask the question without hyperventilating seemed like a minor miracle. "Or plan?"

He released a harsh laugh. "We need to face facts, honey. I'm not good marriage material. I've been straight with you about that from the start."

"Are you saying you want . . . ?" She couldn't complete the sentence.

His mouth compressed into a grim line. "I suspect you'll be the one asking for a divorce." Apparently, he didn't have the same qualms as she did about using the word. His arms tightened around her in direct opposition to his comment. "You've always longed to be part of a family, even though you've hesitated to fully commit until recently. I've been part of two. My mother, who died. And my military unit, who also died. Being part of something means depending on them and trusting them. It also means unfathomable pain when you lose them. I can't go through that again."

She stared in disbelief. "And you believe if we marry, or rather, stay married, that you'll lose me?"

"I almost did lose you," he shot back. "Benedict came within an inch of taking you out."

"Almost, Ty. Almost." She rested her head against his shoulder. "I'm still here and I'm not planning on going anywhere. And in case it escaped your notice, I've also been part of a family that fell apart. I've also known violence, if not on the level you experienced it. Now tell me why you're putting up roadblocks that don't exist."

"I've always been a lone wolf, Lucia," he warned.

She didn't cut him any slack. "That's bullshit. You *were* a lone wolf. But wolves mate for life. And whether you realize it or not, that's what you've done with me. Wolves also form packs. That test says you're part of the Dantes' pack."

He tensed. "Let's just say I'm better off staying on the outside looking in."

"Why?" She pulled back to look at him. He averted his gaze, his jaw clenching for an endless moment and she pushed a little harder. "I'm not letting go of this. Tell me why you're pushing me away."

"It's safer," he whispered. "You can't get hurt if you don't let people in."

"Ty." She waited until he fixed his gaze on her. His words should alarm her. Instead, they filled her with compassion and a strange understanding. "Don't you get it? We're both on the outside looking in, and we're outside because we're afraid to take a chance. Maybe, just maybe, we'd be better off stepping inside. You know your true identity now, and that means you have a choice to make. In or out? Because if you're in, I'm right there with you."

"And if I'm out?"

She offered a slow, loving smile. "Then I'm right there with you, assuming you'll let me."

He squeezed his eyes closed and his throat convulsed. Finally, he spoke. "Lucia, I have a confession to make."

"Tell me."

This time when he looked at her, his eyes were unshuttered, his gaze direct and filled with an emotion she didn't dare name. "I love you, sweetheart. I'm madly, passionately, desperately in love with you."

Oh, God. Her eyes burned and she fought to keep from breaking down. "Are you sure?" She couldn't prevent a tear from escaping. "Because I love you, too."

"I know."

What? "How do you know?" she demanded.

He kissed her tenderly, a hint of hunger bleeding through. "You told me on our wedding night."

Her eyes widened. "I did?"

"And then you fell asleep before I could tell you that I loved you, too."

Lucia glared at him in exasperation. "And you couldn't find another opportunity anytime over the past two weeks to 'fess up?"

A slow smile played across his mouth, a mouth he put to excellent effect once again, taking her under in a slow, passionate kiss. "It had to be the right moment," he murmured against her lips.

She softened. "And this is the right moment?"

"Can you think of a better one?"

She snuggled close. Could today get any better? Maybe, just maybe it could. "Does this mean we're staying together?"

"That's what it means."

"Even if we have to marry again?"

"Even if."

Okay, she wouldn't get a better opportunity than this. She steeled herself to introduce the next topic of concern, thrusting aside nerves. "So, there's one more issue we should discuss."

He lifted an eyebrow. "Uh-oh. Is it a deal breaker?"

"Could be," she admitted.

"Aw, hell." He released his breath on a long sigh. "Tell me."

Perhaps she should find a way to ease into the discussion. No sense in panicking him right from the get-go. "It occurs to me, we've never discussed children."

"Making them or practicing to make them?" She caught the teasing tone underscoring the question.

She cleared her throat. "Both. Maybe more having them, since we've gotten pretty good at the practicing part."

Especially in the shower and hot tub, which is where, she suspected, their daughter had been conceived. And maybe one or two other times when passion had caused their brains to misfire when it came to using contraception.

He offered a wicked grin. "I'm in favor of both making and practicing to make."

"And actually having them?" she dared to ask.

"The more the merrier," he answered promptly. "In fact, you might want to get started on that. I'd like six. Maybe seven. I'm thinking, purely from a logistics standpoint, it would be faster if you'd do it two at a time."

No question he was joking. She'd see how long he kept laughing when she dropped her little bombshell. "Okay. Could we start with one?"

"Sure, if you insist."

"Would it be okay if it's a girl?"

"Why not? I'm an equal opportunity father."

"That's good, because Nonna says it's a girl."

"Nonna says what's a girl?"

"Our baby."

For such an intelligent man, it took him a moment to connect the dots. "You buried the lede, sweetheart," he rumbled. He pulled back, his expression growing serious. "Nonna thinks you're pregnant?"

"Yup. That's what she told me today."

He released a sigh of relief. "Her eye, again? That's what we're talking about, right?"

"It's a pretty accurate eye." He stilled in that predatory way of his. "Yeah, that seems to have caught your attention."

"My full attention." His gaze slid downward, settling on her abdomen. Ever so gently he cupped her there. "Are you pregnant, my sweet wife?"

"That's what the test says. Two pink lines."

His brows drew together. "Two pink lines mean it's a girl?"

She bit back a laugh. He'd asked so seriously, clearly having no idea how pregnancy tests worked. "No, just pregnant. One line means not cooking. Two lines means ding-ding-ding. Bun is in the oven. Nonna's the one claiming it's a girl."

He swallowed. "A daughter." The word escaped rough and hoarse.

Her brows shot up. "You believe Nonna?"

"Let's just say I've learned not to bet against her."

"Ty, are you sure? Sure about us, I mean? Sure about our marriage?"

He drew in a deep breath. "Is that why you didn't tell me about the baby when I first came home?"

She waved a hand in the direction of the clothing scattered haphazardly around them. "You distracted me," she temporized.

"And maybe you waited in order to see if I planned to commit to our marriage?"

"Ty, *I'm* committed to our marriage. I didn't tell you about the pregnancy because I didn't want you forced to stay with me because of the baby."

He didn't hesitate, his words firm and absolute. "Looks like we're both committed to our marriage."

"Then the only remaining decision is whether we choose to walk through the door and become Dantes or walk away. And that's entirely up to you. But, my brother will always be in my life," she cautioned.

"I'd never ask you to give up your brother for me, any more than I'd expect you to turn your back on your Dante relatives."

Relief flooded through her. "What about your relatives?"

He shook his head. "I don't know. I don't even know if they're interested in meeting me, let alone accepting me into their family."

He was breaking her heart. "Chances are they'll want to at least meet you. And I suspect they'll let you take the lead in any future relationship. None of what happened is your fault. They know that."

"And I know it, too. At least, my head does."

"I suspect they're far more concerned about you accepting them than the other way around."

"My grandparents are still alive," he admitted. "And they have a brood as large as your Dante family."

"Then, I guarantee, they'll want to meet you. And I also guarantee, your grandparents are probably terrified of how you'll react to discovering you're a Dante." She kissed him, then kissed him again, whispering against his mouth, "They're the ones standing on the outside, Ty. Will you let them in?"

His response was a long time coming, but more from his inability to speak than resistance to her question. "I'll let them in."

"And my relatives?"

"I'll walk through that door with you." His huge hand returned to cup her belly. "We'll all walk through that door."

Before she could respond, her new cell phone chirped. She glanced at the caller ID. "It's Sev."

"Take it."

She didn't bother with a conventional greeting. Something told her, it wasn't good news. "What's happened?"

"It's bad, Lucia," Sev said, confirming her fears. "The two of you need to get to the hospital. Fast. They've rushed Nonna into surgery."

6 Months Later . . .

Ty and Lucia stood at the gravesite hand in hand. Stooping, he set the bundle of flowers in front of the maker, running his hand over the rough granite.

"Ty, would you mind if we named the baby Julietta after Nonna?"

He rose and wrapped an arm around her, the other resting on her swollen abdomen. "I think that's a perfect name, all things considered."

She tilted her head back. "You don't mind that we're not naming her after Candice?"

He shook his head. "No."

"Is it because of what she did? Or because you've decided to change your name to Dante?"

"It feels . . . inappropriate." He glanced at the marker. "I think she'd understand, don't you?"

"I do." She leaned against her husband, or soon to be husband. She found the precise legalities confusing. "I suspect in the end she was sorry."

He nodded, and Lucia sensed he no longer experienced the anger he had following that long-ago meeting with Primo. He'd come to accept his past, which was good since he couldn't change it. "And the ring she gave me did lead to the truth."

"Are you ready to meet your grandparents?"

He drew in a deep breath and blew it out again. "Confession time. I admit, I'm a little nervous."

"They're probably a lot nervous."

He lifted an eyebrow. "What about you? Can you handle getting married again?"

"I think I can handle it, although it'll be strange calling you Romero, instead of Ty." Her brow wrinkled. "Or maybe Rom?"

"You can call me anything you want, sweetheart. For you, I'll answer to any name you choose." He held her with a calm, serious look. "Are you prepared to finally become a Dante?"

She gave it some thought. "Wishes are funny things, aren't they? I've always longed to be a Dante and now that it's happening it feels—"

"Surreal?"

She shook her head. "Right."

"I'm glad." He turned back toward the grave and once again stroked the marker. "Goodbye, Mom. I forgive you for taking me away from my family. And I thank you for taking such good care of me. But it's time for me to go home now, where I belong."

Tears filled Lucia's eyes as he turned his back on his past and faced his future. A future where they'd never again be on the outside looking in. A future where they'd always belong. A future where their lives would begin anew.

They arrived at the church a few minutes late. Cars filled the lot and they ended up parking in the overflow section. Ty grabbed Lucia's hand and tucked it in the crook of his arm. When she made to rush, he slowed her to a walk.

"They can't begin without us," he teased.

"I don't like keeping everyone waiting."

He deliberately paused in the middle of the parking lot and pulled her close. His daughter bumped against him, giving an energetic kick. He grinned at the sensation and lifted his wife's face to his. With great deliberation, he kissed her, gently easing past her lips and sinking in deep. Her response came as it always did, instantaneous and helplessly passionate. She'd never been able to resist him, any more than he could resist her.

Satisfied for the moment, he took her hand and climbed the steps to the church. Sunlight followed them inside, brightening the dim vestibule. His gaze shot to the two couples sitting on a bench, quietly chatting. At their advent, four pairs of eyes swiveled in his direction. Two rejoiced. Two were filled with nervous joy.

Primo and Nonna stood. While Lucia's grandfather now managed without a cane, Nonna still required one, though she'd made huge strides since the night she'd been so critical and everyone had been called to the hospital in anticipation of her passing. She'd surprised them all, fighting to remain with Primo and the rest of her family. And though her recovery had been long and arduous, she was almost back to normal.

Lucia's grandparents approached, offering swift hugs and kisses, before beckoning to the couple hovering nearby who appeared to be a decade or so younger.

Primo made the introductions. "Romero Dante, may I present your grandparents. This is Ursino, and your *nonna*, Contessa."

A huge bear of a man, as tall and broad as Ty, regarded him with a fierce, black gaze. Dear God, it was as though he stared at an older version of himself.

"He looks just like you," Lucia whispered in awe.

"There is no mistaking the relationship," Ursino concurred in a deep, rumbling voice, a Texas accent mingling with the lyricism from his Italian heritage. "You are my grandson. You must call me Bear as do all my grandchildren."

Contessa looked as beautiful and regal as her name implied. She wore her pale, silvery-blonde hair in a stylish knot, a pair of wire-rimmed glasses perched elegantly on the tip of her nose. Huge blue eyes regarded him warily. Ty would have described her as self-contained if not for the single tear that rolled down her cheek. "You are my poor Silvio reborn," she murmured.

For the first time in his entire life, Ty didn't know how to react to a situation. Bear took the decision out of his hands, sweeping him into a powerful hug and slapping him on the back so hard it almost staggered him. He'd have Lucia check for dents after the ceremony. Following suit, Ty hugged his grandfather in return, though not quite as hard, at least not hard enough to leave dents. Then he did the same with his grandmother, wrapping her up in a gentle, tender hug, before kissing each cheek. Finally, the older couple embraced Lucia, exclaiming excitedly over her pregnancy bulge.

"Thank you for coming," he said, once the introductions were completed.

"Did you doubt it for one minute?" his grandmother asked in disbelief.

"You are our miracle," Bear added.

Contessa caught Ty's hand in hers. "The entire family has come to witness your marriage. Our Romero Dante has returned to us. And instead of keeping the name you thought was yours, you have chosen to become one of us." She spoke with unmistakable passion, struggling to control the emotion that echoed through each and every word. "We would never have asked such a thing of you and yet you give it to us freely."

"All of your aunts and uncles are here, as well as all of your cousins," Bear added. "Down to the very last one."

For some reason Ty's throat closed over. Fortunately, Lucia stepped into the breach. "We're honored to have you."

"You must show us your brand," Bear insisted.

Lucia shook her head in confusion. "I'm sorry? My *brand?*"

"Your mark." He grasped her right hand in his and turned it palm up. "Ah, you have the Dante D brand. It is common amongst eldest sons."

Ty stared at the mark decorating his own palm. Well, hell. How had he missed it? What they'd been calling a stylistic half-moon was clearly a scripted D. He grinned. Go figure.

"Come," Bear encouraged, slamming him on the back again, coming within inches of dropping him. "The three of us will go in. We shall sit and you will take your place at the altar. Then your bride will enter with her grandparents and we will all witness your marriage."

"You do know we're already married, right?"

"Ty Masterson was married. Romero Dante is not," Bear retorted. "We will correct that today, yes?"

Ty inclined his head. "Yes, we will." Pausing long enough to give Lucia a lingering kiss, he joined his grandparents.

To his shock the groom's side of the aisle was filled to overflowing. He'd never had relatives before. Now he had more than he could count. After escorting his grandparents to a seat in the first pew, he stood in front of the altar and turned to watch his bride walk down the aisle, her grandparents bookending her.

He didn't think he'd ever seen anything more beautiful or more moving. He'd never been an emotional man, at least not until he'd met his Inferno bride. She approached, love gleaming in her glorious teal eyes. She'd worn her hair long and it curled and bounced in celebratory abandon around her hips, framing the baby she carried. She paused at his side and he took her hand in his.

The ceremony passed swiftly, solidifying his new identity, as well as Lucia's. Romero Dante. He was Romero Dante now. And she was Lucia Dante. Now and forever more. Where once they'd both stood alone and outside, they were now and forever joined. To each other. To their family. To the generations that preceded, and those soon to be born.

This time the priest remembered to tell him to kiss the bride, which he did with gusto. All around them Dantes cheered.

But it was Primo who put it best. *"Per sempre uno,"* came his powerful shout, one echoed on both sides of the aisle. *"Per sempre famiglia. Per sempre Dante!"*

For that's what they were and would always be.

Forever one.

Forever family.

Forever Dante.

I can't thank you enough for taking the time to read *Forever Dante: Lucia.* It's because of you that I can spend my days writing more stories for your enjoyment. If you liked the book, would you consider leaving a review? Reviews help authors gain new readers on Amazon and that in turn allows me to continue writing more books. Thank you!!